REVENGE OF THE SPAGHETTI HOOPS

BY MARK LOWERY

The Roman Garstang Adventures

The Jam Doughnut that Ruined My Life
The Chicken Nugget Ambush
Attack of the Woolly Jumper
The Great Caravan Catastrophe
Revenge of the Spaghetti Hoops

Charlie and Me: 421 Miles from Home

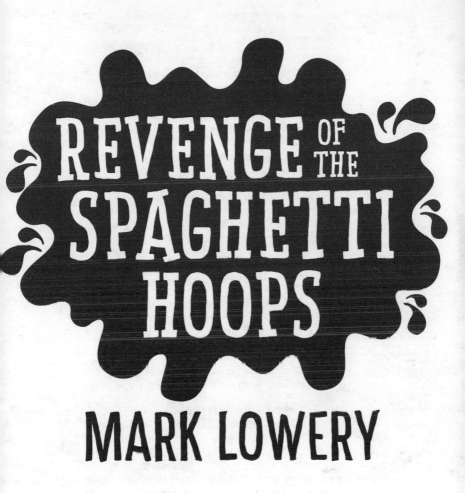

REVENGE OF THE SPAGHETTI HOOPS

MARK LOWERY

Piccadilly
PRESS

First published in Great Britain in 2018 by
PICCADILLY PRESS
80–81 Wimpole St, London W1G 9RE
www.piccadillypress.co.uk

A CIP catalogue record for this book
is available from the British Library.

ISBN: 978-1-84812-729-6
also available as an ebook

1

Typeset by Palimpsest Book Production Ltd, Falkirk, Stirlingshire
Printed and bound by Clays Ltd, St Ives Plc

Piccadilly Press is an imprint of Bonnier Zaffre Ltd,
a Bonnier Publishing company
www.bonnierpublishing.com

To Sar, Jam, Sam and Ol

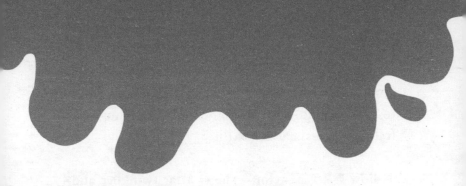

A lot of people wish they were famous.

They dream of being singers, movie stars, YouTube vloggers or people who hold the world record for peeling bananas with their ears.

They dream that one day magazines and the internet will be full of stories about who their new boyfriend is, or what kind of cheese they like, or how they lost loads of weight by only eating soil.

They dream that everywhere they go people will recognise them: photographers snapping away as they leave the house, fans mobbing them as they ride their bike, total strangers begging them for selfies as they try to use a public toilet.

It sounds like a nightmare to me.

Rosie Taylor in my class (AKA the worst person

who has ever lived ever) is totally desperate for fame. Last Christmas, her dad paid for an aeroplane to fly around the whole country, pulling the following message behind it:

Follow @RosieTaylor – she is a far twinklier and more beautiful person than you or anyone else you know #queenofcelebrities

But the message was so long and flappy that, during take-off, it got caught in the wheels of the plane and ripped in half. As a result, people looked up into the sky that day and saw an aeroplane flying past, pulling a tattered banner behind it that read:

Follow @RosieTaylor – she is a far t

She got a million followers within just a few hours. Unfortunately, she was so upset by all the rude messages and comments she received that she had to close down all her social media accounts and start again. You can probably guess the kinds of things that people sent to her, so I won't repeat all of them here. My favourite was 'Are you friends with Donald Trump?'

But that's the problem with fame. No matter how hard you try, you can't really control what you're famous for. One of my (two) friends, Darren Gamble, got on the national news last year after he broke into a hospital and tried to steal a dead person.

Yes, that's correct. A dead person.

Luckily, the dead person was actually just asleep in his wheelchair, and he woke up screaming before Gamble could drive him off in a stolen ambulance.

If that's the kind of thing you have to do to be famous, then it's not for me. In any case, I hate the thought of people knowing who I am. All I've ever wanted is to have a quiet life and to be left alone.

Unfortunately, what I want and what I get are very rarely the same thing.

My name's Roman Garstang, and my final week of school was ruined by a famous person. Oh, and some evil spaghetti hoops, but I'll tell you about *them* later.

End of Term

It was my last week in Year Six. My plan was to leave primary school without any fuss:

Clear my tray.

↓

Give Mrs McDonald that manky three-year-old box of chocolates from the back of the cupboard that nobody will eat because the label's in Russian.

↓

Go home.

Have a few doughnuts to celebrate.

Set fire to my uniform in the back garden, while dancing around the flames in my pants.

You know, all the usual stuff.

No drama. No stress. No excitement.

But it didn't work out like that.

I know what you're thinking: *why* didn't I want a fuss? *Why* am I so bothered about having a quiet life? Leaving primary school is a big deal. Any *normal* person would want to celebrate and have a party. I must be about as much fun to be around as a sack of diarrhoea.

I don't care if people think I'm boring. I *want* my life to be boring. I've had enough excitement recently. In the last few months I've:

- shaved a guinea pig,
- caused a flock of old people to riot,
- been weed on inside a giant floating plastic ball,
- had a flying badger fall in love with me,
- and been in a stolen car as it dragged an exploded caravan through a field with a naked man hanging off the back.

See. If you were me, *you'd* want a boring life too.

In fact, there was only one thing I was looking forward to during the whole of my last week at school.

What I REALLY wanted

My school has a brilliant tradition. It's called YEAR SIX RANDOM MENU WEEK. During the last week of the school year, the Year Sixes who are leaving get to choose what everyone in the school eats for lunch.

So, the week before, the school cook came into class and got each of us to write down our dream lunchtime menu. She said that she'd cook the best ones, but we had to be sensible. Most people wrote boring stuff like cheeseburgers and hot dogs. Gamble put 'roadkill kebabs'. Rosie Taylor's suggestion was: 'Mince up Roman and turn him into meatballs'.

I think that I came up with the absolute best choice of all, even if I do say so myself:

MAIN COURSE
Sausage, baked bean and cheese doughnut
DESSERT
Raspberry jam doughnut

Oh yes. Double doughnut.

I *love* doughnuts. And when I say I *love* doughnuts, I don't just mean I love *eating* doughnuts. I mean that my dream is to one day marry a lady-doughnut and have a whole bunch of human-doughnut children.

After all of the terrible things that'd happened to me recently, I'd completely stopped eating any other food. Mum was getting worried. Apparently, it's a 'bad thing' if you eat thirteen doughnuts a day and nothing else.

So, a few weeks before the end of term, she'd started stuffing all of my meals inside doughnuts so I would eat more. It sounds strange but it worked!

I'd gobbled down meat pie and mash doughnuts. I'd stuffed my face with roast dinner doughnuts. I'd even eaten a salad doughnut (although I *had* picked out all of the salad first and replaced it with jam. I'm not mental).

But the best one of all – the ultimate, most super-sonic, world champion doughnut meal – was the sausage, baked beans, cheese and jam doughnut.

This might seem horrible but let me tell you, it is DEEEELICIOUS (even better than a raspberry jam doughnut, and *that* is saying something)! Imagine: all the sweet, fluffy joy of a doughnut, mixed with cheesy, beany, sausagey goodness. Seriously, it's probably the greatest thing ever invented. Better than the wheel. Better than the internet. Better than the beard.

And if you don't believe me, try one! The recipe is simple:

1.   Take six jam doughnuts.
2.   Slice three of them in half. Scoop out the jam and some of the dough.
3.   Save the jam. Eat the dough.
4.   Stuff each hollow doughnut with a sausage and a spoonful of beans.

5. Put the top half of the doughnut back on.
6. Spread the jam on top and sprinkle with grated cheese.
7. Put under the grill until the cheese and jam start to bubble.
8. Eat.
9. Have the other three jam doughnuts for dessert.
10. Try not to explode with happiness.

Yum-yum. Lovely.

A double doughnut and some quiet time: were they too much to ask for from my last week at school?

What do you think? This *is* me we're talking about.

MONDAY

Morning

We Become Famous and Gamble Uses the Swimming Pool

'So, Year Six,' cooed Mrs McDonald, my teacher, 'welcome to your final ever week at primary school!'

Everyone cheered.

Well, apart from Miss Clegg (Darren Gamble's teaching assistant). She didn't just cheer. She jumped up on her chair and started singing: 'Oh yeah! Five more days and he'll be gone forever!'

Miss Clegg is meant to look after Gamble and keep him out of trouble, but she hates him and she's completely useless at her job. Last month he drank the ink out of the school photocopier and she didn't try to stop him or anything. In fact, she even sat down to watch with a bag of popcorn and said: 'Oooh. This should be good – that stuff's *extremely poisonous.*'

'Miss Clegg, please,' said Mrs McDonald.

'Oh, sorry!' grinned Miss Clegg, who was now robot dancing. 'Got carried away.'

She flopped back down in her seat to reveal Gamble sitting next to her. His little bald, peanut head was twitching up and down, and two filthy rivers of tears were pouring down his face. I hadn't seen him this upset since the school confiscated his samurai sword.

'Darren. What's wrong?' asked Mrs McDonald, concerned.

Miss Clegg sniffed. 'His pet maggot probably ran away cos it couldn't stand the smell.'

'No!' wailed Gamble, 'I'm upset cos I don't want to go to high school in September. I want to stay here with you, Mrs McDonald, cos I love you!'

I felt sorry for Gamble. He sounded so sad and sweet and delicate. But then he ruined it by turning back to Miss Clegg and growling, 'So shut your gob, you big, hairy gorilla's boob!'

'Oh, Darren. I'll miss you too,' said Mrs

McDonald, trying to ignore the last bit. Gamble gets away with loads of stuff, otherwise Mrs McDonald wouldn't have time to breathe. 'But don't worry. You'll still have your friends. Like Roman.'

I forced a smile. Gamble is fifty per cent of my friends. Despite everything, I do kind of like him, but he does scare me a bit. He's like a puppy that can hop on to your lap and lick your face one minute, then suddenly bite you or go to the toilet in your shoes the next.

And yes, Gamble actually *does* do all of those things.

Gamble bashed his desk with his fist. 'You're right, Mrs McDonald. At least I'll have my best mate, Roman. We'll be together forever!'

Before I could move, he'd jumped out of his seat, scrambled across two tables, dived on top of me and clamped on like one of those blobs that live in rock pools.

'I'll never let you go, Roman!' he howled.

'Great,' I croaked, trying not to breathe through my nose.

Miss Clegg looked at me. 'You'll have to get the army to blow up your jumper after that filthy little beast's been near it.'

Normally, Gamble would've retaliated at this

comment, but Mrs McDonald distracted him by asking, 'Who wants to hear our big news?'

Darren jerked his head back, leaving a sticky slug trail on my jumper. 'Are we allowed to smoke cigarettes in class from now on?'

'Er . . . no,' said Mrs McDonald.

He let go of me and tramped back to his place, muttering, 'What's the point of being here?'

'Are we finally going to bury Roman alive?' asked Rosie Taylor, the worst person in the world. 'You can get this stuff that'll totally dissolve his body in three days. There'll be – *like* – nothing left of him. Hashtag: *as if he never existed*.'

'Oh, stop being horrible Rosie,' said Vanya Goyal, who was sitting next to me.

Vanya is the other fifty per cent of my friends. She's a lot better than Gamble though.

In fact, saying that Vanya and Gamble are my best friends is like saying that my two favourite foods are 1) doughnuts and 2) spiders that drop into my mouth when I'm asleep. I.e. one's lovely and I really like them, the other one's disgusting and I don't have any choice over them at all.

'Yeah, Rosie, stop being horrible to Roman or I'll bite your eyes off,' said Gamble.

Rosie pursed her slug's bum mouth and folded her arms across her new black-and-white fur coat.

'*Ahem*, Rosie,' said Mrs McDonald, 'is that jacket school uniform?'

Rosie rolled her eyes. 'Course not. It's panda fur.'

Mrs McDonald's eyes nearly popped out of her head. 'What? As in *real* fur from a *real* panda?'

'Er. I think that's what *panda fur* means,' replied Rosie in an *OMG-how-dumb-are-you* voice. 'Daddy bought it to cheer me up after Roman ruined my cousin's wedding.'

I said nothing. A week before, my cousin had married Rosie's cousin. Rosie had completely disgraced herself at the wedding. She'd stolen my dad's car and driven it right through the crowd, while dragging the smashed-up caravan and naked man behind it.

Apparently, you're not meant to do this at someone else's wedding.

Somehow this was all *my* fault, though, and since then she'd been worse than ever.

'You *do* realise that pandas are an endangered species, don't you?' said Vanya. 'People shouldn't be making jackets out of them.'

Rosie snuggled into the coat. 'I *did* feel bad about the panda at first. But it *is* a gorge-tabulous jacket. Plus we used its eyelids to make super-cute earrings so it *like* didn't die for nothing. Hashtag: *it's what it would've wanted.*'

There are no words to describe how dreadful she is.

'But about this news . . .' I said, starting to feel a little bit on edge. 'Is it the Random Menu? Do you know it yet?'

'No,' said Mrs McDonald, 'you'll find *that* out each day at lunchtime.'

Lunchtime?! How could they make us wait that long? My belly would've shrivelled up and fallen out by then.

Vanya squeezed my arm. 'Don't worry, Roman,' she whispered, 'I'm sure your doughnuts will be on there.'

I smiled as bravely as I could. She always knows how to cheer me up.

'The news is even more exciting than that,' said Mrs McDonald.

Yeah right, I thought. Nothing could be more exciting than a double doughnut. Not even a baby with a moustache.

She continued, 'You may remember we sent a letter home to your parents a few weeks ago, asking if you were allowed to be filmed for something.'

We all looked at her blankly. Nobody reads the letters that get sent home. Normally I shove them in my bag and wait for Mum to dig them out a few days later.

Mrs McDonald pointed towards the door. 'Line up, everyone. Miss Clegg – put Darren into his reins. This is going to be the most incredible last week of term EVER.'

Oh No No No No

Out on the playground, the big gate on to the road was wide open. This explained why Gamble had to wear his reins. The last time someone left a gate open, he tried to run away to Canada to 'live among the wolves'. He got as far as the local park, where he was found farting on a one-legged pigeon.

There were three people waiting for us on the playground: two women and a man. One of the women had a camera on her shoulder. The other was holding a long pole with a furry microphone on the end.

The man had an iPad in his hand. He was wearing an open-neck shirt and jeans, and his long hair was dragged back into a ponytail.

'Hey, guys!' he said, grinning at us. 'I'm Trevor.'

'O to the M to the G!' announced Rosie Taylor, leaping in front of the camera. 'Is she filming us? Are we on TV? Hi, fans. It's me – Rosie Taylor!'

The camerawoman sniffed. 'No. It's not on yet.'

Rosie tutted. 'What's the point of having a camera if you're not beaming pictures of Rosie Taylor around the globe? Hashtag: *give people what they want.*'

'Well . . .' continued Trevor, 'I'm sure Mrs McDongle told you . . .'

'McDonald,' said Mrs McDonald.

'Please don't interrupt,' said Trevor, his smile twitching slightly with irritation. He seemed like the kind of person who gets stressed out easily. '*You* are going to be starring in your very own TV show. We're filming it this week and hopefully it'll be on telly next month.'

The whole class went crazy-wild. People were dancing around and hugging each other. Rosie began slapping on make-up. Gamble strained at his reins, eyes bulging and mouth foaming like a rabid dog. Kevin Harrison was so excited he ran straight to a bin with his hand over his mouth. Of course, Kevin is always throwing up, which is why his nickname is Ali Blargh Blargh and the Forty Heaves.

'Before we start,' said Trevor, calming us down, 'there are six rules for making the perfect TV show. Number one: act natural.'

'*Natural?*' asked Gamble, 'You mean strip off naked and that? Cool.'

A few people giggled.

I didn't. I knew he wasn't joking. Gamble is always whipping off his clothes. Like when we went to the cinema together and he 'felt hot' during the film. It was bad enough that he was nude. But he absolutely did *not* have to run down the aisle and do a handstand right in front of the screen.

'No. As in, don't show off. Pretend the camera's not here.'

He was saying this to Rosie Taylor, who was posing and pouting her lips. I think she was trying to look beautiful, but she looked more like a squid that was suffering from painful wind.

'So . . . *why* are you filming us? What's so special about our last week at school?' asked Vanya Goyal.

Vanya is always asking questions. She likes to understand everything. I sneaked a smile at her. I'm proud that my best friend is the smartest, coolest girl in the class.

'Aha!' said Trevor, pulling his mobile out and speaking into it. 'And roll.'

A red light on the camera began to flash. Moments later a car pulled through the gates and on to the playground.

Well, I say 'car'. It was actually a highly polished, jet-black stretch limo – as long as four normal cars – with tinted windows and purple neon lights along the bottom of the doors.

'OMG!' said Rosie. 'It must be a famous person. That American actor Marlon Grunt has six of these – one for each of his pet chimps.'

A celebrity?

Hmmm.

I only know one celebrity and, trust me, he was the last person I wanted to see. A horrible feeling grew in my belly as the car glided across the playground and purred to a halt in front of us.

Then I saw the registration plate: GR00V35.

My skin puckered into goosebumps. My stomach churned.

Oh no no no no, I thought. *Please not . . . him. Anybody but* **him.**

The back door opened and smoke billowed out of the car. At first I thought it was on fire, but then I realised that it was stage smoke, designed to make a big entrance.

'Children,' said Mrs McDonald, 'meet your new classmate. Or should I say, your *old* classmate . . .'

And that's when I knew that my worst fears had come true.

'Oh, nuggets,' I said.

The smoke cleared to reveal a small, skinny boy with an enormous mop of curly hair. He was wearing a pair of skin-tight leather trousers with chains and buckles hanging off them. His purple velvet shirt was open all the way down to his belly button, showing off a shark's-tooth necklace. Perched on top of his hair was a ridiculous hat with a feather sticking out of it.

Jason Grooves.

I did not need this in my life right now.

Apart from me, everyone else cheered. Jason spun round six times on one foot, then pulled his hat down over his eyes and shrieked: 'YOOOOW!'

The cheering got louder.

Gamble fell to his knees and bowed down in front of him. 'We're not worthy!'

'Yes! A fellow celebrity!' exclaimed Rosie Taylor. 'Finally, someone else who isn't a completely scuzz-tabulous, talentless tramp.'

I shuffled behind everyone else, hoping that he might not see me.

Jason Grooves took off his hat and ran his hand through his enormous hair. 'What's up, my brethren? JG's back in the house.'

As he said this, his piercing blue eyes met mine, and he stared directly at me. 'Hello, Roman,' he said eventually. His voice was cold and unpleasant, like an ice cube down the back of my trousers.

I gulped.

Jason Grooves

Here's all you need to know about Jason Grooves:

- He used to go to our school until last year.
- His real name isn't Jason Grooves; it's Kenneth Shufflebottom.
- He changed his name when he went on *Britain's*

Really Talented (or *BRT*). This is the biggest thing on TV: a massive talent show with all sorts of comedians, dancers, acrobats, magicians and everything else.

- Jason's a singer and dancer, and he's **REALLY** good. Everybody in the country thought he was one super-cool little dude, which is why he changed his name. Super-cool little dudes cannot be called Kenneth Shufflebottom, no matter how good they are at singing.

- He had to leave our school halfway through the series because his fans were crowding round the gates every morning, trying to get pictures with him and ripping off chunks of his uniform to sell on eBay.

- He reached the final of the whole competition, which was amazing. Everyone in the school went in to watch it in the hall, even though it was a Saturday night. It was really exciting – we all had banners and flags and T-shirts, and people from the TV show came to film us.

- The only two acts left at the end were him and a juggling sheep called Boris. The sheep couldn't actually juggle by the way. It just stood there, while its owner hid behind a black sheet and stuck her arms out under its body. It was pretty funny but also a bit lame. Everyone was certain that Jason would win.

– But he didn't win. He came second. This was a massive shock to the whole country. Oh, and I should say it was a little bit my fault.

What happened was this:

There were about five minutes to go until the voting lines closed. We were all nervously watching on the big screen in the school hall.

The head judge – Simon Bowel – was onstage with Jason Grooves, Boris the juggling sheep and Boris's owner. The presenters – Nat and Ned – said that the votes were neck and neck, and that they were going to pay one more visit to see the two finalists' fans.

First, they went to a man in a field with a load of sheep. The sheep didn't really have anything to say, apart from *baaaaa*.

Then they went to see Jason's fans – in other words, us.

As soon as they started filming us, everyone went totally crackers – leaping up and down, screaming, waving flags. Kevin *Ali Blargh Blargh* Harrison was sick into someone's special Jason Grooves hat. It was chaos.

Finally, the reporter pointed a microphone at the nearest person.

Unfortunately, that person was Rosie Taylor.

'Hi, fans!' she trilled. 'Actually, I'm more talented than Jason and Boris put together, so vote for me inst–'

The reporter wrestled the microphone off her and shoved it at the next person.

Unfortunately, *that* person was me.

'Tell the twenty million people at home what you think about your classmate, Jason Grooves,' she said.

The room hushed. The camera was right in front of my face.

I was struck with nerves. 'Well. I. Erm . . . *Twenty million?* Wow . . .'

The whole nation was watching and waiting but my mouth was dry and my mind blank. There was a long, painful silence.

The reporter motioned for me to speak. Meanwhile, I had Rosie trying to shove me out of the way, and Gamble on the floor next to me, violently yanking on my trouser leg and hissing:

'Just tell her a joke. Have you heard about the man with five willies . . . ?'

And that's when it happened.

Rosie gave me one last push, which caused me to half spin round and trip over Gamble. I fell forward on to my hands and knees.

Unfortunately, Gamble was still yanking on my trouser leg. As I fell, he pulled them right down round my ankles.

The whole country was given a view of my big, shiny bottom.

And that was that. It turned out that people didn't want to vote for someone whose fan pulled a moony on national TV. There was a late surge of votes for Boris the juggling sheep and Jason did not win.

Boris won a hundred thousand pounds and the trophy. Boris got to perform for the Royal Family at Christmas. Boris was on TV with his owner every five minutes. Boris was the main act on the *BRT* tour. And Boris got a movie made of his life.

Meanwhile, I had to go into hiding and didn't leave home for three weeks. There were TV and newspaper reporters camped outside my house, until they all got fed up and found something else to write about. It took me months to get over it.

I hadn't seen Jason Grooves since that night.

Handshake

Back in the playground, Jason stared at me with his cold eyes. Everybody else noticed, and they all shuffled out of the way so there was a clear path between the two of us. At the edge of my vision, I could see the camera pointing at me.

Slowly, a smile spread across Jason's face and he held out his arms. 'Hey, Roman, don't sweat it, man. I ain't still mad with you.'

Relief flooded through me. 'Oh, thanks. I was wor-'

'No hard feelings,' he said, 'Trust me, I blame the sheep one hundred per cent. C'mon. Let's hug this out.'

He strutted over and grabbed me. Even though he was being friendly, there was something about how tight and how long he hugged me that made my blood feel like it was turning to frozen jam.

Then he looked over my shoulder. His face

suddenly lit up and he exclaimed, 'No way! It's the V-Machine! Come here, babe!'

To my horror, he was talking to my best friend Vanya.

The V-Machine? I thought. *Babe?*

There was something I didn't like about this.

It got worse. They started doing a handshake.

And not just a normal handshake either – one of those ones that lasts about six weeks. Their hands were a perfectly-synchronised blur of clicks, slaps, finger-wiggles, wrist-flicks and thumb-spins, finally finishing with a kind of jazz-hands pretend-explosion thing.

'Smashed it, V!' said Jason, before turning back to the rest of the class. 'Yo. Who wants to know what it's like being famous, aieee?'

I stood there as Jason led everyone back indoors.

'How cool is this?' Vanya asked me, clapping her hands together. 'I can't believe he's come back. Jason and I used to be best friends. We went to street-dance club together for years.'

'Oh, that's nice,' I said, trudging behind her towards the classroom.

There was a strange feeling in my belly. It was like I'd come home and found someone in my

kitchen, wearing my pyjamas and eating my doughnuts.

Love Interest

In the classroom, we all sat down. Jason plonked
himself on Mrs McDonald's desk. 'Mind me sitting
here, big M?'

Big M.

Mrs McDonald waved her hand to say *fine*. If
I'd sat on her desk like that, she'd have set her pet
guinea pigs on me.

'OK,' said Trevor, 'you can ask Jason anything.
But we're filming this, so remember, we have six
rules for the perfect TV show. One . . .'

He put his hand behind his ear and everyone
called out: 'Act natural.'

Trevor gave the thumbs up. 'And rule two . . .
keep it exciting! Roll camera!'

Rosie put her hand up straight away. 'Do you
have a girlfriend?'

Everyone giggled. Jason clicked his fingers. 'I
know lots of girls.'

'Do you *want* a girlfriend?' said Rosie, more
forcefully.

'Well . . .'

'Can I be your girlfriend?'

'Er . . .'

'Can we get married? How many children do you want? I want six. Their names will be: Rosie, Rosie 2, Handbag-Blingerella if it's a girl or Billy-Bling-Bob if it's a boy, Rosie 3, HashtagMillionaireDiamondStyle. And instead of a name, the last one will just have its own emoji.'

Good grief.

'Ha ha, cut,' said Trevor, 'And that's the third rule for the perfect TV show. Make sure there's a love interest.'

'What's a love interest?' I asked.

'You know,' said Trevor, 'two people who like each other.'

A few people made *kissy kissy* sounds.

'Obvs I'll be Jason's love interest,' said Rosie Taylor. 'Some people say I'm the prettiest girl in Europe.'

I tried not to laugh here but I couldn't help it. I don't want to be cruel but Rosie has a face like a chewed sausage.

She glared at me. 'This is my big chance of fame, Roman. Don't you dare ruin it.'

'We'll decide on love interests later. Next question,' said Trevor, trying to move on.

Gamble shouted out, 'Oi, Jason. Do you want me to beat up Boris the juggling sheep for you?'

Mrs McDonald pinched the top of her nose.

'What a nut-job,' sighed Miss Clegg.

Jason Grooves suddenly looked very cross. 'Yo. I'd like that a lot. That sheep is a sweaty little butt cabbage and the only reason it beat Jason Grooves was because . . .'

'Cut!' said Trevor, looking a little annoyed. 'We've talked about this, Jason. You can't moan about the sheep during your TV show. We *need* the people watching at home to like you. And they won't like you if you complain about the sheep. Rule four of a great TV show – *we need to like the hero*, remember. People hate people who hate animals.'

'Woolly-brained fool,' muttered Jason under his breath. 'Couldn't even juggle.'

Wow. He really did not like that sheep.

There was a long silence, then Vanya put her hand up. 'I *still* don't get why you're filming us.'

Trevor smiled patiently and motioned for the camera to stop. 'Well. Everyone in the country loved Jason on *BRT*.'

'For real,' said Jason, which I think meant *yes they did*. He was calm again now that people were talking about how great he was.

'But,' continued Trevor, 'unfortunately, he didn't win the final.'

Jason frowned. 'Thanks to that sh—'

Trevor raised an eyebrow to shut him up. 'The sheep's been all over the TV and internet ever since. People might've forgotten how amazing Jason is.'

'*We* haven't forgotten,' smiled Mrs McDonald.

'Thanks M-Dog,' said Jason.

M-Dog!

Mrs McDonald gave a wiggle of excitement.

'So **that's** why we need the TV show and **that's** why it has to be amazing,' continued Trevor. 'If we make a bad show, it won't get on to the TV. So who's gonna make this the best TV show ever?'

Everyone cheered.

'Who's gonna do exactly what they're told at all times?'

Everyone cheered again.

I didn't cheer though. I didn't like this at all. *What did he mean by 'do exactly what we're told'?*

'I still don't get it,' I said.

Trevor sighed. 'We're going to release Jason's first music album in a few months. Before then, we've got to remind the world how great he is. People will watch this TV show, fall in love with him again, listen to his music, go to his concerts, buy his cuddly toys.'

'Cuddly toys?' I asked.

'Boom!' nodded Jason. 'I got a range of personalised merchandise, all available on my website – Jason Grooves toys, Jason Grooves bubble bath, Jason Grooves T-shirts . . .'

'Jason Grooves toilet roll?' I offered.

I thought this was an OK joke but there was total silence. Then Jason laughed coldly. 'Very funny, Roman. You're a funny guy, you know that?'

Trevor seemed to think about it though. 'Hmmm. Toilet roll. We're always looking for new products . . .'

'What's the TV show going to be called?' asked someone.

Trevor clicked his fingers and pointed. '*Jason: Grooving On as Normal*. It's all about how Jason's going back to school. We need to show what a nice, normal kid he is.'

'Normal?' asked Rosie. 'Who wants to be normal?'

Trevor shrugged. 'Nobody likes a show-off. Remember rule one of a great TV show: *act natural*.'

Rosie slipped off her panda-skin jacket.

'I'm still a normal kid, just like you,' said Jason.

At that moment his phone rang and he whipped it out. It was a golden iPhone – the latest model – with *JG* written in diamonds on the back.

'We don't allow ph–' began Mrs McDonald.

Jason silenced her by holding up a finger. 'I gotta take this. It's Simon Bowel.'

'*Oooooh!*' said everyone.

I mentioned Simon Bowel earlier. He's the head judge on *BRT*. You know, the guy with the square head and the hairy chest, and the trousers pulled up to his armpits. Everyone in the country knows him.

Normal kid?

Jason didn't seem too normal to me. Normal kids don't ride in stretch limousines, or have TV shows made about them, or take calls from famous TV stars.

Or start doing handshakes with other people's best friends, for that matter.

'OMG!' cried Rosie. 'Jason knows Simon Bowel. Hashtag: *I HAVE to marry him now.*'

Jason winked at her as he chatted quietly on the phone at the side of the room. Rosie made a strange gurgling noise like a blocked toilet.

'Simon Bowel's paying for this whole TV show,' explained Trevor, 'and he's giving the school loads of money to film here. He'll decide if the TV show is good enough to be on telly. So he's the boss of all of us.'

He kind of laughed at this, but it seemed like he didn't really find it funny at all.

Helicopter

'Right then,' said Mrs McDonald, 'first lesson is swimming. The pool's being drained tomorrow for the summer, so this will be your last ever lesson here.'

Most people went *awwwwww*.

I didn't. I'm not a big fan of the school pool. It's freezing cold and the size of a shoe box. Plus, I'm about as good at swimming as a broken sofa with Miss Clegg sitting on it.

'Did you say, *drained tomorrow?*' asked Gamble.

Mrs McDonald squinted at him. 'Yes, Darren. Why do you ask?'

Miss Clegg sniffed. 'I expect cos it's the only bath he ever gets.'

This was probably true, but it wasn't nice. 'Shut your gob, you stinky old toilet-snorkeller,' snapped Gamble.

'Swimming?' said Trevor to Mrs McDonald, flicking through notes on his iPad. 'You didn't say anything about that. Jason hasn't brought his kit.'

'You can borrow my undies, Jason,' said Darren, 'I'll go commando.'

'You know, I'm all right . . .' said Jason.

'It's fine,' said Trevor, a little stressed. 'I'll call for the helicopter to bring his shorts over.'

Jason nodded. 'Simon Bowel said I could use his chopper anytime I wanted.'

'How cool's that?' said Vanya to me. 'I've never been in a helicopter before.'

Huh, I thought, *Just a normal kid in his normal helicopter.*

'You can have a ride in it sometime, V,' said Jason.

Vanya smiled and Rosie glared at her.

We had to wait for the helicopter for ages. In the meantime, we had to listen to Jason's stories about the *BRT* tour. He and the other acts from the show had spent the last six months performing every night in front of thousands of people all around the country.

'I felt the love of the crowd every night,' he said. 'But you wanna know what really sucked?'

'What?' asked Rosie, who was leaning so close to him that she was practically inside his mouth.

'That dumb sheep!' he cried, suddenly mad. 'It got its own bus to travel on. It got the best dressing rooms. Everyone treated it like a god, but–'

'Jason,' growled Trevor through gritted teeth. 'Rule four – *we've got to like the hero.*'

Every time Jason mentioned the sheep, his eyes would flick to me and it made me feel really uncomfortable. 'I don't like the way he keeps looking at me,' I whispered to Vanya.

'You're imagining it,' she said. 'He told you he's forgiven you for what happened.'

Hmmm . . .

Maybe she was right. Maybe it *was* just the sheep. Maybe he wasn't still angry at me.

I wished I could believe her.

Swimming

Eventually, the helicopter landed on the school field and dropped off Jason's swimming trunks. I have to say this was pretty amazing, although the moment was ruined when Gamble threw Miss Clegg's coat into the spinning rotor blades and shredded it into a million pieces.

After it flew off, we finally gathered our stuff together, headed over to the pool and got changed.

Miss Clegg has to go into the water with Gamble during swimming lessons. This is ever since he climbed up on top of the changing sheds and did a wee down on to everyone below. She doesn't like wearing a swimming cossie in front of us though, so she always wears a wetsuit. I don't want to be horrible, but she's got quite a large, lumpy body. Nobody looks good in a wetsuit, but Miss Clegg looks like a bin-bag full of coconuts.

The pool is above the ground, so you have to go up a little ladder to get into it. While everyone else lined up, Miss Clegg climbed the steps.

Gamble was behind her. He was wearing massive goggles, three pairs of armbands, a rubber ring, and – instead of trunks – an old pair of undies.

They might've been white once but they were now a kind of yellowy-grey colour, like three-day-old snow at the side of the road. When Miss Clegg reached the top step, he shoved her in the back and she went sprawling into the pool.

'You little brute,' she spluttered at him.

Gamble splashed water at her face. 'Ah, stop busting my melon, mega-bum.'

Miss Clegg ducked her head underwater. She does this a lot during swimming lessons. I think it's so she can swear at Gamble without being heard.

Jason was the last one out of the changing shed. His swimming shorts went all the way down to his ankles, and he was still wearing his shark's-tooth necklace.

'Yo man. I'm super-pumped about this,' he said to the camera. 'It's awesome that we could get the helicopter out here.'

Gamble called out: 'Hey, look! I can do an impression of a helicopter. Do you think I'd get on *Britain's Really Talented*?'

Without thinking, the camerawoman turned to film him. She regretted this straight away. 'Oh, that is horrible!'

Mrs McDonald let out a scream. 'Darren Gamble!

Pull up your underpants right now and stop swinging your will–'

Luckily, we were spared Gamble's vile impression by a blood-curdling yell from inside the swimming pool.

'YEEEEAAAAAARGHHHH!!'

Everyone spun around.

The pool was a frothing mass of bubbles, with Miss Clegg in the middle of it all. 'HEEEEELLLLLLP!' she cried, flailing her arms and struggling to stand up.

Gamble pulled up his undies. 'Forgot to say: *don't go in the pool, innit.*'

'She didn't really have a choice,' I said.

'They're eating me!' howled Miss Clegg.

'*Who's* eating you?' asked Mrs McDonald, panicking.

Miss Clegg let out another yelp, then shot into the air, before crashing back into the water and soaking everybody around the side of the pool.

What was going on?

'Someone DO something!' wailed Mrs McDonald, as Miss Clegg fought to keep her head above water. The pool is quite shallow but the bottom is really slippery.

I leapt into action.

Well, by 'leapt into action' I mean that I stood there and did nothing.

I wish I *had* leapt into action though, because what happened next would lead to some very serious consequences.

You're SOOOOOO Brave

'She could die here!' said Trevor, who seemed surprisingly happy about this. 'Excellent! This'll look great on TV. Go for it, Jason!'

Jason Grooves ran up to the side of the pool and vaulted cleanly into the water. He disappeared for a moment, then emerged holding Miss Clegg under both of her chins.

With a few powerful arm pulls, he dragged her safely to the steps, then vaulted back out again.

'You're SOOOOOO brave!' sighed Rosie. 'Please marry me.'

'Nice one, Jason,' said Vanya, giving him a high five as he walked past.

Jason shrugged. 'JG loves saving lives.'

'I was about to dive in too,' I said, realising how pathetic I sounded.

Meanwhile, Miss Clegg was lying on the patio area by the side of the pool, panting like a faulty Hoover. 'AAARGH!' she shrieked. 'It's still on my toe!'

She flicked her foot. Something flew off the end of it, sailed through the air and smacked into the side of the swimming pool.

Gamble scurried over and scooped it up. 'There there, my pretty one. Don't be scared,' he said, plopping whatever it was back into the pool.

'Darren. What is going on?' demanded Mrs McDonald.

Gamble scratched a spot on his bald head. 'My fish tank's got a leak, cos I headbutted it yesterday, so I had to put my pet fishies in the swimming pool.'

'You did *what?*'

'I had to, miss. To keep 'em alive while I wait for my uncle to steal me a new aquarium.'

I peered over the edge of the pool. There were three dark, broad shapes – each about as long as a ruler – swimming around the bottom.

'What *kind* of fish are they, Darren?' asked Mrs McDonald.

'Just piranhas, miss,' said Gamble.

'Piranhas?!' gasped Mrs McDonald. 'Aren't they deadly?'

Gamble waved her away. 'Nah. They're sweet, miss. Like goldfish. But a bit more bitey.'

'They could've eaten me alive!' screamed Miss Clegg.

'What do you expect?' said Gamble. 'They probably thought you were food.'

In fairness to Gamble, Miss Clegg's feet *do* look a lot like chubby pasties.

Mrs McDonald rearranged her glasses. 'But *how* did you get the fish into the pool?'

'Well, miss,' said Gamble, looking proud of himself. 'I broke in last night, disconnected the CCTV cameras and the burglar alarm, picked the lock on the swimming-pool gate, drained half the pool out, changed the chemicals so it was safe for the fish, refilled the pool, then switched the alarm and the CCTV back on so nobody would know. Simple really.'

Holy moly! Even though this was pretty naughty, you have to say it was quite impressive.

Mrs McDonald's mouth opened and closed a few times.

'I'm gonna crush you for this,' said Miss Clegg,

holding a towel against her bleeding toe with one hand and pointing at Gamble with the other.

She sounded like she meant business.

Two Words

Trevor got a bunch of people to carry Jason Grooves back to class on their shoulders, like he'd just scored the winning goal in the World Cup final.

This was a bit much. All he'd done was save Miss Clegg. I don't want to be mean but there's a lot of Miss Clegg to go round. She wasn't in any real danger – it would've taken those fish *months* to eat her.

'Terrific!' enthused Trevor, as Jason carefully stood up on top of some of the shoulders, then drabbed three times.

In case you've been living under a rock, the drab is a dance move that the whole world's been doing for the last year. You tilt your head to one side and put your hands underneath, like you're pretending to sleep. Then you take them away and do it again. And again. And again.

It was made famous by Jason, who used to do

it on *Britain's Really Talented* every time he got the golden buzzer.

Apart from me, the whole class drabbed back at him. Then Jason backflipped off and landed perfectly on the ground.

'Maybe one of the girls could give him a kiss on the cheek,' said Trevor.

'I will! I'm his love interest!' cried Rosie Taylor, pouncing on Jason and kissing him all over his face. In the end it took three people to pull her off and Jason was all dazed and confused, as if he'd just been beaten up.

'Urgh!' said Vanya. 'Kissing is disgusting!'

I smiled. For some reason, I was delighted that she hadn't been the one to kiss Jason.

'Well,' said Mrs McDonald, once the class had calmed down. 'So this is your last week at primary school. How do you want to spend it?'

Ideas were shouted out from around the room: class parties, talent shows, art projects.

I said nothing. All I cared about was the Year Six Random Menu Week. I sat there, licking my lips and dreaming of double doughnuts, as everybody else made their suggestions.

'Rounders match!' called Vanya.

'Oooh! Good one!' said Mrs McDonald, scribbling it down on the board.

Trevor gave Vanya the thumbs up. 'Rule five of a great show: *rivalry and competition*. Get the audience to cheer for their favourite.'

'How about a lemonade-drinking competition on a bouncy castle?' said Kevin *Ali Blargh Blargh* Harrison.

'Maybe not . . .' replied Mrs McDonald. Kevin only has to *look* at a bouncy castle and he starts throwing up.

'Gladiators,' shouted out Gamble.

Mrs McDonald took off her glasses and squinted at him. 'What exactly do you *mean*, Darren?'

Gamble twitched excitedly. 'Like we learned about in the Romans, miss. Get some hungry wild animals, then we'll all fight each other to the death with daggers and nets and that.'

The room fell silent.

'Er . . . maybe it's time for your computer treat, Darren?' said Mrs McDonald uneasily.

Gamble gets to go on the computer at the back of the classroom every day. It's meant to be a treat for good behaviour but I think it's just a chance for Mrs McDonald to have a rest from him. He seems to be allowed on it every day, no matter what he does. For Gamble, 'good behaviour' just means he hasn't actually chewed off anyone's leg that day.

'Ace!' he said, jumping from desk to desk to the computer. 'I'm a proper good boy, me! I always get my treat.'

Miss Clegg hauled her enormous frame out of her chair and limped after him. 'I'd treat him to a punch in the throat,' she muttered.

'I heard that, you big sweaty camel's nipple,' he said over his shoulder.

Miss Clegg growled at him. 'You just wait till tomorrow.'

That was the second time Miss Clegg had told him to wait for something. Whatever it was, it didn't sound nice.

Trevor clicked his fingers right in front of Mrs McDonald's face. 'Since Jason was such a hero this morning, maybe *he* should choose how the class is going to celebrate this week.'

'Er. OK . . .' said Mrs McDonald.

Huh, I thought, *he'll probably want us to build a statue of him so we can all worship it.*

Trevor whispered something into Jason's ear, then backed away. The camerawoman started filming.

'You know what this class needs?' Jason asked. He paused for about a minute, looking around the room to build up the excitement, just like when the judges announce the winner on *Britain's Really Talented*. Then, as everybody else leaned in to hear him, he whispered two words that would unleash absolute mayhem: 'A prom.'

What's a Prom?

For the third time that morning, the class got extremely excited. Some of the girls were hugging each other. Rosie Taylor was telling everyone she was going to steal her dad's credit card and fly to Italy for a new dress.

'Pretty cool, eh?' Vanya asked me.

'I have no idea,' I replied, confused. I seemed to be the only person who didn't know what a prom was.

'And cut!' called out Trevor. 'Great reaction, kids.'

'Hang on,' said Mrs McDonald, 'I don't think we can just organise a prom like that.'

Trevor took a deep breath and put on one of his super-fake smiles. 'Look. I've told you, Mrs McDoodah . . .'

'McDonald.'

'Yeah, that. We're making a *TV programme*. Rule six of making a great TV show: y*ou need a big finale*. The whole series can build up to it.'

'But it's the children's last week of school. You can't just come in and change everyth–'

Trevor put his finger over Mrs McDonald's lips. 'Simon Bowel is giving the school a lot of money so we can make this show, remember? So do as I say. Now, I need you to ask Jason what a prom is. Do you think you can manage that?'

He said this last bit like he was talking to a particularly thick two-year-old. He wasn't being very nice at all.

Grinding her teeth together, Mrs McDonald glared at the camera. 'What's a prom?'

'Wasn't so hard, was it?' said Trevor.

Jason fluffed up his hair as the camera swung round to him. 'It's a great big glamorous party, y'all. Music. Food. Entertainment. Red carpet. Limos. Everyone's gotta get dressed up nice.'

'And who's going to organise it?' asked Mrs McDonald, folding her arms. She didn't seem quite so keen on the TV show any more.

'JG and Trevor,' said Jason.

'And me,' said Rosie, blowing a kiss at Jason. 'I'll help to make it a night to remember.'

Jason put on his sunglasses and gave a *hey – aren't I good-looking?* smile.

Gross.

I wasn't excited at all about the prom. It sounded like a fancy school disco to me. The last time I went to a school disco, Rosie Taylor put superglue on my orangeade bottle and I had to go to hospital to have it removed from my lips.

At least I had more important things to worry about. For now anyway. It was Random Menu Week. Was today the day of the double doughnut?

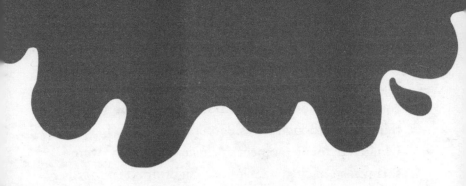

Lunchtime

The Menu Is Explosive, and Jason Does a Runner

At twelve o'clock, I was already halfway off my seat, leaning towards the door. If there were double doughnuts on offer, then I was NOT going to miss out. The moment the bell rang, I burst forward like a turbo-charged ostrich.

'Roman! Stop!' shouted Mrs McDonald. 'We wait till we're told to leave. You can go last.'

Ah, great. I stood there as the rest of the class poured out around me. I don't think she was actually all that annoyed about me rushing out. She was still mad about the prom and I was just the first person she could tell off.

When I finally made my way to the hall, I passed Jason Grooves and Trevor, huddled together in conversation. Jason seemed annoyed about something. Even though I was desperate to get to lunch, I lingered for a moment to hear what they were saying.

'But I thought the TV show was all about me, man,' whined Jason. 'The other one's OK, but why can't I have that one?'

The other what? I thought.

'Look,' said Trevor, 'I'm telling you the audience will prefer the other one. And Simon Bowel said that if the TV show isn't good, it won't get shown and . . . Hey! You!'

They both snapped round to look at me.

'I-I-I didn't hear anything,' I stammered.

Trevor and Jason glanced at each other, then they both burst into smiles.

'Hey, Roman. We're buddies now, remember?' said Jason, coming over and clapping his hand on to my shoulder.

'Yeah!' said Trevor. 'Jason's forgotten all about what happened with your bum during the *BRT* final. Haven't you, Jason?'

For a moment, a little tiny muscle in Jason's eye

twitched. But then he playfully punched me in the arm. 'Course I have, man. It's all the sheep's fault. Let's go eat.'

Is it . . . ? Is it . . . ?

The lunch queue snaked all the way out of the hall and down the corridor. *Typical.* As soon as we joined the back of it, everyone crowded around Jason as if he was a magic doughnut or something. The camerawoman was filming him.

'Do a dance, Jason!' someone called out.

'Excellent!' said Trevor. 'Any chance to show off your skills.'

'I couldn't possibly,' Jason said. He was trying to sound modest, but he'd already kicked off his shoes and handed his hat to Kevin *Ali Blargh Blargh* Harrison. 'Yo! Don't puke in that, Kev!'

'I can't promise anything,' replied Kevin sadly. This is true. He's so used to throwing up into sick bowls that just *seeing* a bowl-shaped object can set him off.

Jason began stretching his neck muscles and limbering up. Everyone else was excited but I couldn't have cared less. Ahead of me, I could see the menu stuck to the hall door. I edged around Jason's audience to get a closer look.

Is the double doughnut on there? Is it . . . is it? Could this be the greatest day of my life . . . ?

Well, what do *you* think?

This *is* me we're talking about, after all.

Two terrible things happened within the space of three seconds.

Firstly, I got close enough to read the menu. My heart sank.

Chicken in creamy sauce and spaghetti hoops. On the same plate.

Gross. It must've been Kevin *Ali Blargh Blargh* Harrison's choice. He always chooses foods that curdle together in his stomach and make him puke.

I was so crushed by the menu that I didn't even bother to read what the dessert was. But then, unbelievably, things got worse.

'Go on. Ask her,' I heard Trevor say behind me.

I turned around. Jason was now standing in the middle of a circle. To my horror, he turned to Vanya. 'You wanna show 'em what we can do, V?'

I didn't like this at all.

Vanya blushed. 'But it's years since we did street dance together.'

'If she doesn't want to . . .' said Jason.

'Nonsense!' said Trevor, gently shoving her into the circle.

Within moments, everyone was clapping their hands in rhythm, while Vanya and Jason spun round on their heads and body-popped and flipped around together, before finally finishing in an arms-crossed, back-to-back pose.

Everyone went mad. Apart from me that is – I felt like someone had sucked out my insides with a vacuum cleaner. Oh, and Rosie Taylor. She glared at Vanya in the same way a crazed penguin might stare at a fish-thief.

This was shaping up to be an awful lunchtime.

But, for me, things can always get worse.

Spaghetti Hoops

The dinner lady slopped a great big ladleful of spaghetti hoops on top of the creamy chicken sauce.

'What's for dessert?' I asked miserably.

'Fruit. Want some?'

Fruit?

I didn't even bother to answer such a ridiculous question. Of course I didn't want any fruit. She might as well have offered me a plate of boiled rats' bums or a bowl of dirty old knickers with rotten-egg custard.

I snatched up my tray and went to find a seat. I wanted to sit with Vanya, but for some reason Trevor the TV guy ushered her to a different table.

I sat down, and was soon joined by Gamble, who decided he was going to suck his lunch up through a straw.

Utterly gross.

I pushed the spaghetti hoops around my plate. They're pretty disgusting things, when you think about it – all sloppy and gloopy and swimming in thick sauce. I held my nose and forced a forkful into my mouth.

As I was chewing, Jason sat down next to me. Trevor stood over us, with the camerawoman alongside him.

'You two buzzed about the prom or what?' Jason asked.

'Definitely!' exclaimed Gamble. 'My brother Spud had a prom at his high school, right, and he ended up burning the whole building down. It was well mad!'

'Oh,' said Jason.

I carried on chewing, the spaghetti hoops swirling round my mouth like worms in a washing machine.

'Psst,' said Trevor to Jason, from behind the camera. 'Ask about the *you-know-who*.'

'Do I have to?' said Jason.

Trevor nodded. 'Yes, you do. Remember Simon Bowel won't put us on TV if the show isn't exciting.'

'All right, all right,' said Jason, taking a deep breath. 'Hey, Roman. You know Vanya, don't you? What's the deal with her? She got a boyfriend?'

What?!

A boyfriend?!!! She's only eleven!

Unfortunately, at this exact moment, I just happened to be swallowing. The shock caused me to snort the entire mouthful of half-chewed spaghetti hoops right up my nose.

It wrecked! My knife and fork clattered to the floor. I clutched my neck and started making weird snorting noises.

'You OK, man?' asked Jason.

But I wasn't OK. My nose and throat were burning. My eyes were watering. I couldn't breathe. My chest started convulsing. And then . . .

AAAAAACCCCCCCHHHHHHOOOOOOOO!

I sneezed.

Right into Jason's face.

Not just a normal sneeze either. This was enormous. A volcanic eruption of half-chewed lumps of spaghetti hoops and tomato sauce that shot out of my nose and mouth and sprayed across his face.

'Interesting reaction . . .' said Trevor, looking at me and rubbing his chin.

Jason stared at me in horror. His whole head was completely splattered.

'I am *so* sorry,' I said, dabbing at his face with my sleeve. 'I just . . .'

'What did you do that for, you disgusting fr–'

'Jason!' said Trevor. 'Remember! Be nice to the little jealous kid.'

The *what*?! Me? Jealous? Eh? What did he mean by *that*?

I didn't have time to ask him though, because Gamble leaned across and peered really closely at Jason. 'Hey!' he said. 'This bit of spaghetti looks just like my uncle Terry.'

He plucked a lump of mangled pasta off Jason's cheek and held it up to the light. Funnily enough, he was right. There were two or three bits of hoop all mushed together. And the way they'd been chewed and sneezed out made them look like a big fat head with a nose, a mouth and even an eye.

'Brilliant!' Gamble grinned, tossing it into his mouth.

'That's the most horrible thing I've ever seen,' Trevor said.

Gamble swallowed. 'The snot definitely adds an extra bit of chewiness.'

'Aha! Another thing to mention tomorrow,' said Miss Clegg, who was hovering around in the background like a giant bug. 'Darren's a revolting ape with no manners and normal people shouldn't have to look at him.'

'Hang on,' said Trevor, who was wiping Jason's face. 'What did he just say?'

'About the snot?' said Gamble. 'It's well good – like free chewing gum.'

'No. You said the pasta looked like your uncle.'

'So what?' said Gamble.

Trevor pulled Jason to his feet. 'Quick. We gotta get out of here. I've got an idea. I'll explain on the way. Someone tell Mrs McDingaling we won't be back till tomorrow.'

With that, he ran out of the dinner hall with Jason following behind.

TUESDAY

Gamble Finds Out about His Future and We Have Another Visitor

That night I woke up at 3 a.m. from a terrible nightmare:

It was the night of the *BRT* final. Straight after the trouser incident, a giant snake with big fluffy hair burst into the hall. It ate Vanya whole. I could see the shape of her as she passed along its body.

The whole time, she was doing the drab. Then everyone else turned into Trevor, and they were all filming me and drabbing and opening their snake mouths to eat me and –

I woke up in a cold sweat and had to go downstairs for an emergency doughnut.

I hadn't been able to get back to sleep after that for ages. My mind was racing with worry about Jason, Vanya and all those strange threats that Miss Clegg kept making to Gamble.

Because of all this, I was dazed, confused and late when I got to school on Tuesday. I would've had the day off sick if it wasn't for the possibility of double doughnuts being on the menu.

I certainly wasn't ready for what I saw when I finally arrived in class. Darren Gamble was clinging to the leg of his table while Miss Clegg tried to drag him out of the room by his ankles. 'I AIN'T GOING!' he yelled. 'So get off me, you ginormous bum wizard.'

Miss Clegg prised his fingers off one by one. 'I've told you. You've GOT to be there.'

Gamble started squealing and lashing out with his feet and elbows, until Miss Clegg dropped him with a thud. He lay on the floor, glaring up at her.

'What's his beef?' said Jason Grooves, strutting past me into the room and drabbing the class. Trevor and the film crew were behind him.

'She's making me go to some stupid meeting,' said Gamble.

Jason sighed. 'Sounds rough, bruv. Would it help if I sang you a song?'

I wasn't sure how this was going to help, but Jason jumped on to a desk anyway. 'This track's off my new album. I wrote it myself. It's called "My Lady Love".'

Trevor tapped the screen of his phone. Tinny music came out of the speaker, then Jason began to sing. Obviously, he's got a good voice, but the song was HORRIBLE. The words were all soppy, and I think he'd just written anything as long as it rhymed. E.g.

'You'll be my princess and I'll be your prince.
You'll be my onion and I'll be your mince.'

And:

'You make my heart explode,
Every day since we met, my love for you has growed.'

And:

'I'll buy you a packet of Skittles from Spar,
You make me feel like ooh ooh ah ah ah.'

You make me feel like ooh ooh ah ah ah?
What does that even mean? He sounded like a monkey in a hot bath. What next? *You love me, I love you. Bah bah oink oink moo moo moo?*
Pathetic.
But nobody else thought he was pathetic. In fact, when he'd finished warbling, everyone drabbed, clapped and cheered like he'd just saved a rucksack full of kittens from a fire.
Jason looked directly at the camera and winked. 'Available soon on CD and download.'
Trevor gave him the thumbs up. 'Rule seven of this TV show: *we've got to advertise Jason's music.*'
Rule seven? How many rules were there? I thought there were only meant to be six.
'I remember all the rules,' simpered Rosie. 'Act natural . . . have a love interest (AKA: me) . . . make sure people like the hero . . . rivalry and competition . . . and have a big finale. Now can I be Jason's girlfriend? Hashtag: *rule eight – marry me.*'

Jason opened his mouth but Trevor spoke over him: 'Jason hasn't decided who his girlfriend will be yet.'

Decided? I thought, *Don't the girls get any say in it?*

'I'm sure you'll make the right decision, Jason,' said Rosie.

'What's that song got to do with Gamble?' I asked, totally confused.

'OMG, Roman,' said Rosie Taylor, 'you are soooooo stupid. That song wasn't about Gamble. It was obviously about me.' She gave one of her horrible slug's bum smiles. 'I love you too, Jason Grooves. We'll be a celebrity couple, like Melissa Slump and Jeremy Badge. AKA: *Sludge.*'

She blew a kiss at Jason, but Trevor actually pushed him out of the way, so it missed and went at me instead. Even though it was invisible, it gave me a grim, cold feeling on my cheek, like I'd been breathed on by a dead person.

Rosie looked furious. 'Urgh! Disgustamungtabulous. My air kiss hit Roman. I literally feel like pulling my lips off.'

I said nothing.

'Ah, Jason,' said Mrs McDonald, folding her

arms. 'Lovely singing. But why weren't you here yesterday afternoon?'

Trevor answered for him. 'Big news. We'll tell you tomorrow.'

'You can't just walk out whenev–' began Mrs McDonald.

Trevor raised a finger. 'Not cool, Mrs McDillydang. Your job's to make Jason look good, got it?'

'I thought my job was to teach,' said Mrs McDonald.

Trevor shook his head. 'Just remember how much money the school is getting for this TV show.'

For a moment, Mrs McDonald stared at Trevor, her face turning redder and redder. In fact, it might even have turned purple, if Miss Clegg hadn't suddenly screamed, 'Get down here NOW!'

While our backs were turned, Gamble had piled four chairs on top of his table, punched a hole in the ceiling tiles, and was now climbing up into the roof space. His legs were dangling out of the hole and a cloud of dust was showering down.

Miss Clegg made a grab for his ankles and he booted her in the head. 'I'm moving into the loft to live with the bats.'

Just a regular morning for Darren Gamble.

'I could write a song about this,' said Jason.

'No need,' I said.

Mrs McDonald was underneath him now. 'Darren. It's important that you go to this meeting.'

'I'd rather eat my own brain,' said Gamble.

'Small meal,' grunted Miss Clegg.

'Would it help if you took a friend with you?' asked Mrs McDonald, ignoring her.

Please not me, I thought. Gamble is terrible in meetings. One time I was in a school council meeting. Halfway through, he ran in holding a bucket and started throwing live crabs at people. He never explained why.

Gamble dropped on to the table and grinned. 'Roman. He's my bestest friend in the whole wide world. And if he doesn't come I'll pull off his kneecaps.'

Great.

The Sunshine Unit

Miss Clegg led us to the small group room. The small group room is a small room where small groups can go to work. It's not a clever name. A pink-faced, bald man was sitting at the table in there with a clipboard in front of him.

'You must be Darren,' he said to me.

'Wrong one,' said Miss Clegg. 'It's the other weird-looking boy here.'

The **other** *weird-looking boy?* I'm nowhere near as weird-looking as Gamble. The kid's got a head like a sultana.

'Who are you, Baldy?' said Gamble to the man. This was a bit rich coming from Gamble – he looks as if he cuts his hair with sandpaper.

'I'm Mr Gibbons, from Broughton College.'

Gamble stared at him blankly. 'Where?'

I looked at Gamble. *Unbelievable.* 'You know,' I said slowly, 'the high school we're going to in September.'

How did he not know that?

'Well, make it quick,' said Gamble. 'It's my computer treat time.'

Mr Gibbons folded his hands together. 'So Miss Clegg called me, after . . . what happened with the piranhas.'

Miss Clegg looked pleased with herself. 'Told you I had big plans for today.'

I didn't like the sound of this.

'And,' continued Mr Gibbons, 'I've come in to find out more about you.'

'Such as *why are you such a nasty little goblin?*' smiled Miss Clegg. 'And *can you go to a normal high school, or will you have to go to a zoo instead?*'

'It's not a *zoo*,' said Mr Gibbons. 'It's a special part of the school where we can look after children with behaviour issues.'

'What's behaviour issues?' asked Gamble.

'Behaviour issues,' said Mr Gibbons, 'are when children find it hard to do the right thing.'

'In other words, being a right pain in the bum,' said Miss Clegg.

'We take the students with behaviour issues and . . .'

'Chain them up?' asked Miss Clegg hopefully.

'No,' said Mr Gibbons.

Miss Clegg tutted. 'Electrocute them?'

'No.'

'Hang them from the ceiling by their toes and hammer nails into their eyeballs?'

Mr Gibbons shook his head. 'No. We teach them in a separate building so that they can get the help they need, and so that everyone else is safe. We call it the Sunshine Unit.'

'Separate?' said Gamble suspiciously. 'You mean, I ain't going to a normal school next year?'

Miss Clegg smiled at him cruelly. 'Not if I've

got anything to do with it. Once Mr Gibbons sees what you're like, you'll be going to his prison instead.'

'The Sunshine Unit isn't a *prison*,' said Mr Gibbons, 'it's just a separate building. With a high fence. And really strong doors. And bars on the windows.'

It sounded a lot like a prison to me.

'But . . .' said Gamble, his bottom lip trembling and tears forming in his eyes. 'If I go there, I won't be with my bestest mate, Roman.'

'Nope,' said Miss Clegg, who was really enjoying herself now. 'You'll be stuck with all the other horrible little scrutbags like you.'

'Nothing's been decided yet,' said Mr Gibbons. 'And that's why I'm here – to find out if the Sunshine Unit is right for you.'

'It will be,' said Miss Clegg. 'The kid's a gangster.'

'Ah, shut it, you massive fart-cannon,' snapped Gamble.

Mr Gibbons wrote something on his clipboard.

Miss Clegg looked over at it and clapped her hands together. I hadn't seen her looking so happy since that time Gamble fell off the PE shed roof after she'd prodded him with a hockey stick.

Normally I'd never be rude to a member of staff, but there was something about this that made me cross. 'Why are you doing this to him?' I asked her.

'Because he's ruined my life,' said Miss Clegg, 'and I think he deserves to spend the next five years being punished for it.'

'The Sunshine Unit isn't a pun–' began Mr Gibbons, but he was interrupted by the door being thrown open.

Interview

Trevor the TV man burst into the room. 'Right. Out. I need this room.'

'But I'm trying to get this evil little monster locked up for the next five years,' moaned Miss Clegg.

'Hmmm,' said Trevor, setting up a small camera on a tripod and pointing it at an empty chair. 'I think a TV show is a bit more important than some kid's future.'

'Is it?' I asked.

Trevor squinted at me. 'Yes. We're doing interviews with everyone in the class. Asking them about Jason. Helps the people watching at home realise how brilliant he is. Then they buy his music and his merchandise and . . . *kerching* . . . we all get rich.'

'Can I go first?' panted Gamble, bouncing up and down like a deranged wallaby.

Miss Clegg scoffed. 'The only TV show you'd get on is *Britain's Deadliest Scuzzbuckets*.'

Gamble called her a 'butt-sniffer'.

Mr Gibbons wrote something on his clipboard.

'How about *you*?' said Trevor to me.

'*Me*?' I asked.

Trevor gave one of his super-fake fixed smiles. 'Don't worry. Just you, me and this teeny camera. Won't hurt at all.'

So Gamble, Miss Clegg and Mr Gibbons went back to class, while I stayed in the small group room with Trevor. He was right. It didn't hurt at all. But it was very strange.

Trevor started off by asking me a bunch of funny questions, to 'get me warmed up' before the proper interview. It was all silly stuff, like:

Can you describe the stinkiest pair of underpants in the world?

Would you rather have a head like a fish, or be forced to eat a plate of slug brains every morning?

How do spaghetti hoops make you feel?

What would you say if a giant potato man stole your pet hamster, then wanted to be your friend?

And loads more.

I actually quite enjoyed this part of the interview. It took my mind off all my worries about Vanya, Jason and Gamble. In fact, I got carried away and went into tonnes of detail. Trevor was really encouraging, putting his thumbs up and telling me I was doing great.

Then the real interview began and the questions suddenly changed.

He fired them out – *rat-a-tat-tat* – so fast I could barely answer one before he asked me another.

Do you like Jason? Do you want Jason to be successful and famous? How does it make you feel when Jason sings? How would you feel if someone went to the prom with your best friend?

And so on and so on.

After about twenty of them, I felt all dizzy and spaced out, like on that trip to the Egyptian museum

when Gamble hit me over the head with a mummi-
fied cat.

Finally, Trevor stopped and gave me one of his mega-
fake grins. 'Right. Done. I can get rid of you now.'

I didn't like the way he said this. It was kind of
friendly but also a little bit nasty: the sort of thing
a super-villain might say in a film, just after getting
a secret code off you but before feeding you to a
robotic laser-gerbil.

When I got back to class, though, this would be
the least of my worries.

Computer Treat

I walked into the classroom and stopped so suddenly
that Trevor bumped into the back of me.

Jason Grooves was sitting next to Vanya.

In my seat!

They were laughing their heads off about something, while the camera crew filmed them. 'What's
going on?' I croaked, still light-headed from the
interview.

'Oh, hi, Roman,' said Vanya. 'Jason was just
telling me about one of the contestants on *BRT*.'

'Was it the juggling sheep?' I said coldly.

'I told you, bruv!' said Jason, suddenly angry. 'Don't mention that sheep. I swear, if I ever see that nasty ball of wool again, I'll . . .'

'Jason. What have I said?' said Trevor.

Jason folded his arms and stuck out his bottom lip.

Vanya looked crossly at me. 'You shouldn't have mentioned the sheep, Roman.'

'But . . .' I spluttered, 'he stole my seat.'

Then he stole my friend.

'Don't get your knickers in a twist,' said Trevor, ruffling my hair. 'It's all for the TV show. Now. I need another person.'

'Me me me!' cried out everyone in the class.

'Don't interview these talentless peasants,' exclaimed Rosie Taylor, striding over to Trevor. 'You need someone with star quality. Like me.'

I guess Rosie does have *star quality* – in the sense that she's bright orange and I'd prefer it if she was millions of light years away in the middle of space.

'Yeah, man,' said Jason, 'Rosie's broof.'

'*Broof?*' I said.

Ignoring everyone, Trevor checked down a list of names on his iPad. 'Er . . . how about . . . hmmm . . . *Vanya Goyal.*'

He made it sound like he'd just plucked her name out of thin air, but something told me he'd planned it all along. I gulped. What was he going to ask *her*?

'Broof,' Vanya said.

Now she *was saying it too!*

'What does broof mean?' I asked. I'd never heard it before in my life.

'It means *cool*,' she said, before following Trevor out.

They were speaking a new language together! This was definitely NOT broof.

Meanwhile, Rosie's eyes were burning a hole into the back of Vanya's head. I hadn't seen her this angry since that time Kevin *Ali Blargh Blargh* Harrison threw up into her brand new zebra-skin gloves.

Gamble shouted out: 'Oi, Roman. Come on the computer with me!'

I didn't really want to sit with him but, with Vanya out of the room, there were only two other free seats. One was next to Jason (who was singing some crummy song about 'the girl with skin like an angel's wings' – yuck), and the other was next to Rosie. She'd drawn a picture of Vanya and was now shredding it into tiny pieces.

At least if I was with Gamble, it might take my mind off Vanya. Plus I could help him look good in front of Mr Gibbons.

Miss Clegg sat right behind us with Mr Gibbons, talking to him in her boring, yawny voice. I only caught the odd phrase because she didn't want Darren to hear her:

'. . . make sure you write about the time he stole my lipstick and ate it . . .' she moaned, '. . . and when he poured wet cement into that Year One kid's underpants . . . no idea how he caught the mole in the first place, let alone how he managed to staple it to the skateboard . . .'

The whole time, Mr Gibbons scribbled notes on his clipboard.

At this point I decided to say nice things about Gamble. Maybe I could make Mr Gibbons give him a decent report and let him go to the normal school. 'Hey – Darren,' I said loudly, 'remember when you rescued that squirrel with a broken leg from that tree?'

'Really?' Mr Gibbons said, leaning forward. 'What a lovely thing to do.'

It was working.

'Oh yeah, the squirrel,' said Gamble. 'I took it

home then chucked it on the barbecue. Drop of chilli sauce. Nyam. Nyam. *Deeeee*-licious.'

I slapped my hand across my face.

Mr Gibbons cleared his throat. 'Well, Darren. Maybe you can show us what you're looking at on the computer.'

Darren turned the screen around. Things quickly went from bad to worse.

No Unauthorised Access!

The web page was basically a full screen of hundreds of thumbnail photos. All of them were of futuristic-looking weapons or military vehicles: flying armoured cars with rocket launchers on them, giant drones, close-ups of *actual* wasps with mini spy-cameras on their backs, soldiers wearing robotic suits with laser guns on the sleeves.

At first I thought they were pictures from films. Then I noticed something that made the hairs on the back of my neck stand up.

Across the top of the screen, above the photos, it read:

ARMY WEAPON DEVELOPMENT.
TOP SECRET!
NO UNAUTHORISED ACCESS!

I began to feel seriously uneasy. 'What does "no unauthorised access" mean?'

'It means,' said Miss Clegg, 'that this little ratbag shouldn't be on this website.'

'As if I care, you rotten trouser-coconut,' snorted Gamble. 'This site's amazing. It shows all the new weapons the army are inventing. Look – this one's a bomber plane that doesn't need a pilot. It can wipe out a whole city. Here's a sniper rifle that's hidden inside a live chicken. If you click here, you can even find the plans, so you can make your own weapons and test 'em out.'

'But you wouldn't do that, right, Darren?' I said, glancing round at Mr Gibbons and trying to smile. *Maybe I could still help him.* 'You wouldn't *really* create home-made weapons that could injure people or . . . you know . . . *worse.*'

Gamble snorted. 'Course I would! Look at this! It's a special receiver you put inside someone's ear, then you can get 'em to do whatever you want. It's well good! Like a remote control for a person!'

'Oh, wow! I'd love one of those!' said Trevor the TV man, who'd overheard as he came back into the room.

I bet you would, I thought. He wasn't exactly helping the situation.

'Proper easy to build,' said Gamble. 'Look – here's the plan. All you need's a hearing aid, a mobile phone and a few other bits.'

I held my head in my hands. *Why could Gamble not act normally for ten minutes?* He was supposed to be showing Mr Gibbons that he wasn't too naughty for a normal school. And here he was learning how to build deadly weapons on a secret website.

'How did you find the website, Darren?' asked Mr Gibbons. He didn't seem cross like Miss Clegg or terrified like me. It was more like he was interested to find out.

Gamble sniffed. 'I just hacked into the army's secret network.'

He tossed this out casually, as if he'd said, *I just went on to YouTube to look at videos of cats falling over.*

Mr Gibbons squinted at the screen. 'Hmmm. How *exactly* did you do that?'

'I'm well good at hacking into websites, innit. It's one of my hobbies. Along with kicking people.'

At that moment, the bell for playtime rang and he sprinted outside before anyone could stop him.

Top-secret Weapons Testing

Outside, I couldn't find Gamble anywhere. On the far side of the field, the camera crew were filming a group of people who were surrounding Jason Grooves. Now and again Jason would perform a little dance for them. As well as Rosie Taylor and Kevin, the group included Vanya.

I decided I should go over and make sure everything was OK. Not because I was jealous of Jason stealing my friend, you understand. Just because of . . . well . . . some other important reason I hadn't thought of yet.

I'd only gone two steps when a skipping rope suddenly looped over my stomach. It was pulled so tight I could hardly breathe. Before I knew it, I was being dragged backwards. 'Let's play Top-Secret Weapon Testing together,' said Gamble into my ear.

He said 'together' but actually it was more like Gamble played *against* me. First, he tied me to the football posts with the skipping rope. Then he spent fifteen minutes pretending to attack me with different weapons that he'd seen on the army website, in a bid to find out 'which one's deadliest, innit'.

He punched me repeatedly in the arms (rapid-fire machine gun), then he climbed up on to the crossbar and jumped off on to my head (high-altitude heat-seeking bomb), before rubbing grit into my eyes (radar-disabling laser system).

The worst thing was that Mr Gibbons watched the entire thing, scribbling away on his clipboard but not doing anything to save me. I know he was there to observe Gamble's behaviour, but come on! When *exactly* would he have stepped in to help? When I stopped breathing? Or would he have waited till I was actually fully dead?

I begged Gamble to stop so that he wouldn't get a terrible report from Mr Gibbons (and also so he'd stop hurting me). But, as soon as I said this, he unleashed the most deadly weapon of all. This was the 'total annihilation gas grenade', which involved him pinning me down and farting into my mouth until I nearly fainted.

I think he'd made that one up.

I was ten minutes late back to class. By the time I hobbled in, my eyes were bright red and blurry, I had four ice packs strapped to my body, and I was pretty sure there was a hole burned into my lungs.

It's quite amazing, then, that I actually managed to feel worse *after* I got back into the classroom.

Make Sure It Goes OFF!

I flopped into my normal seat next to Vanya. She looked me up and down. 'Does it hurt?'

'Only when I breathe,' I replied.

'Sorry, Roman. I'd have wrestled him off you but . . .'

'You were busy,' I said.

Vanya looked hurt. 'Don't be like that.'

I sighed. 'Losing your best friend isn't *broof*.'

'Yo, man,' said Jason, moonwalking past me. 'Just so you know, nobody says *broof* any more.'

'But you were saying it twenty minutes ago,' I said.

'Things change fast,' he replied. 'Don't want you to sound like a krungle. We say *snife* now.'

Vanya shrugged. 'It's true.'

Krungle? Snife? I give up.

A little smile was curling up at the corners of Jason's mouth. He was making fun of me, I knew it.

Just then, Trevor came in and stood at the front, looking nervous. 'Right, guys. I've just been talking to Simon Bowel. He isn't happy with what I've told him about the TV show so far.'

'What?' cried Jason. 'You mean we might not get it on the TV?'

Was it bad that I felt happy about this?

'But then Jason won't be famous!' said Rosie. 'And neither will I! And we'll never get to have our celebrity wedding! Hashtag: *the world is ruined.*'

Trevor held up his palms. 'Remember rule two. We've just got to *keep the TV show exciting*! So how can we spice this week up, guys? Give me ideas.'

Mrs McDonald seemed cross. 'I think it's exciting enough already. We're having a rounders match on Wednesday. Not to mention the special menu this week. Then there's a leavers' assembly, and . . .'

'An assembly?' said Jason. 'Great! I'll sing!'

I'd rather you didn't, I thought, but everyone else seemed really excited and started drabbing like itchy rabbits.

'It's more about sharing memories of our time at school,' said Mrs McDonald.

Trevor shrugged. 'Don't care. What else might make the week special?'

Miss Clegg danced into the room. I hadn't seen her move this quickly since she was barging Key Stage One kids out of the way to get to that cake sale last year.

'It's already special enough for me,' announced Miss Clegg. 'Mr Gibbons has just gone back to the high school. And *that* little criminal is going there to look round his new kiddy prison tomorrow!'

She pointed gleefully at Gamble, who made a rude sign at her with his fingers.

'Rosie Taylor has an idea for the prom,' announced Rosie. 'Everyone has to go in couples.'

'You mean, like boyfriend and girlfriend?' I cried, in horror.

'That's what I'm talkin' 'bout,' said Jason Grooves, clicking his fingers and pointing at Rosie.

'Great idea!' said Trevor, putting his thumbs up. 'The audience will love it! Rule three: *love interest*.'

'The children are too young for that,' protested Mrs McDonald, but Trevor pretended not to hear her.

The rest of the class seemed delighted and embarrassed at the same time. There was a whole new round of giggling, chatting and drabbing, and people gossiping about who their partners were going to be.

'And the best couple can win a prize,' continued Rosie.

'Fantastic!' said Trevor. 'Rule five: *rivalry and competition.*'

Rosie gave a smile like a really smug turtle. 'They can get crowns, and maybe win a prize and then they can kiss each other . . .'

Trevor rubbed his hands together. 'Prizes. Kissing. Perfect! Rule six: *the big finale!* This'll make great TV! Simon Bowel will love it! I'll get on it straight away.'

Rosie Taylor licked her lips.

'Mrs McDonald, you can be my date, miss, cos I love you, miss,' called Gamble.

Mrs McDonald looked terrified.

At that moment, Kevin *Ali Blargh Blargh* Harrison stepped in front of my table. 'Will you go to the prom with me, Vanya?' he asked.

'Oh. Er. Sorry, Kevin. I've not decided who to go with yet,' she replied politely. I felt a little relieved about this, for some reason.

Kevin moved straight on to Rosie Taylor.

Rosie's face dropped. 'I'd rather go to the prom with your leaky sick bag than with you. Hashtag: *no chance*, Vomasaurus Retch.'

Vomasaurus Retch! Even though this was cruel, it did fit Kevin quite well.

Kevin immediately went to the next girl.

'I've got my eye on someone much better,' said Rosie after he'd gone, staring at Jason.

But Jason wasn't looking back at her.

He was talking to Trevor and looking directly at Vanya, my best friend. I felt my blood run cold.

The Day of the Double Doughnut?

Amazingly, the day just got worse and worse from there.

First of all, there was lunchtime. I went into the hall hopeful and excited. *Maybe today would be the Day of the Double Doughnut?*

But it wasn't.

Nope.

Unbelievably, it was spaghetti hoops again.

Apparently, a second person had put this down as their menu choice, and – *would you believe it?* – the cook had chosen it. Spaghetti flipping hoops two days in a row, swilling around my plate like a big glob of intestines.

At least they were only a side order today, along with a hot dog. And I managed to build a wall of chips so they didn't make the bun soggy – a bit like when people pile up sandbags before a flood.

I was on a table with Vanya, Gamble and Jason (yuck). The camera crew came over and Trevor asked us to 'do something fun'. Jason leapt up on his seat and sang Vanya a song all about his pet kitten with a wonky leg, which made her look like she was about to cry and made me want to throw up. Then Gamble picked up his plate of spaghetti hoops and tipped it over my head.

'Thanks a bunch,' I said, seething as the slimy spaghetti hoops slithered down my bright red face. The camera was pointing at me, and everyone in the hall was laughing.

'Soz, Roman,' he grinned. 'Couldn't help myself.'

And he wonders why he might be going to a school for naughty kids.

I was in the toilets for ages, washing sticky, gloopy sauce out of my hair. There were even lumps of spaghetti hoops in my ears. When I came out,

Trevor was standing in the corridor, chatting on his mobile. 'No, Simon,' he said.

Simon Bowel! I thought. *Wow!*

'Jason wanted the other one but I've persuaded him,' he continued. 'All under control. And he's getting something out of it, so he's happy now. Yes. All set for tomorrow lunchtime. Nope. Nobody knows. Top secret. I promise you – the show will be great.'

He turned around at that moment and I had to dart back into the toilet, so I wasn't seen.

What was he on about? That was twice I'd over-heard him mention 'wanting the other one'. He and Jason had been saying that yesterday outside the classroom. And what did he mean: *Jason was 'getting something out of it'?* Most importantly of all, what was all this about tomorrow lunchtime? I hope he didn't expect us to do something. There was no way I was going anywhere. It might be Double Doughnut Day.

It took ages till he'd hung up and gone away. As a result, I was late back into class again.

And that's when the day got even worse.

When I came in, I found Jason Grooves sitting next to Vanya, in my seat!

Again!

Trevor smiled at me. 'We thought it'd be best if Jason sat here for the rest of the week. Make it a permanent switch.'

I looked at Vanya, my mouth hanging open.

'It's just for a few days,' she said.

Yeah! The last few days of school ever.

'It's snife. I'll take care of her, man,' said Jason Grooves, cheerfully winking at me. He was loving it that I was angry.

I flopped into the chair next to Gamble.

'Brilliant!' he said, elbowing me in the ribs. 'My best mate's sitting next to me, innit! Guess what. I'm gonna build that brain controller this week. I can use it on that Mr Gibbons, see, then he'll let me go to normal good-boy school with you next year.'

'Are you sure about that?'

'Oh yeah. I've got the plans. The only thing I don't have is a hearing aid, but I'll easily nick one. You can be the first person I test it out on.'

He said this like it was a really kind offer.

'You know, I might let someone else have a go,' I said. Gamble would be the last person on earth who I'd put in charge of my brain.

'Suit yourself. I'll put it in Miss Clegg's ear instead. Then I'll make her strap some meat to her fat head and chuck herself into the tiger cage at the zoo.'

Miss Clegg looked up from her phone. She seemed to be playing Angry Birds under the desk. 'I'll tell Mr Gibbons you said that tomorrow.'

Gamble ground his teeth together and punched himself in the forehead a few times.

'Can't wait to take to you to the Sunshine Unit,' grinned Miss Clegg. 'You can meet all the other prisoners. I mean pupils. No, actually, I *do* mean prisoners.'

I gulped.

This week was lurching from one disaster to the next.

WEDNESDAY

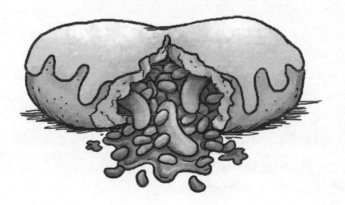

Gamble Is Useful and I Am a Terrible Human Being

Tuesday night had not been good.

I was already worried about Vanya, Jason and Gamble. And then I had to deal with my mum.

I haven't really talked about my mum much. She's pretty much the most embarrassing person of all time. Honestly, when I went to Broughton College for my taster day last month, she insisted on holding my hand right up to the front door and giving me a great big kiss in front of everyone. Then she went up to one of the older girls in Year Eleven and asked if she'd 'show my baby boy where the tinkle rooms are in case he gets caught short'.

Absolutely horrible.

Anyway, the moment I got through the door after school on Tuesday, she grabbed me in a tight hug. 'Oh, my little Roman soldier is all grown up!'

'What *are* you talking about?' I said.

'I got the email from the school about this prom!' she sang.

Great. I'd been trying to keep it a secret from her. 'I don't think I'll be going.'

'Nonononono!' she said. 'You *are* going. The email said it's compulsory. Everyone has to go.'

'Eh? When did they decide that?' I asked.

Mum clapped her hands. 'And the best bit is, you have to go with a girl too. Oh, my little man, out on his first date. We'll need to get you a suit. And we'll have to take some photos. It'll be sooooooo cute. Who are you going to ask?'

'I hadn't really thought ab–'

'How about Rosie Taylor?'

WHAT? I'd rather go to the ball with Darren Gamble. In fact, I'd rather go with Gamble's dog

Scratchy, which is the only creature on the planet more disgusting than Darren himself (imagine Darren but with four legs, patchy fur, breath that could melt a pound coin and a severe case of bum worms).

Then it dawned on me. I was going to have to ask someone to the prom. I hadn't even considered it up until then. I suddenly felt cold and unpleasant, as though Frosty the Snowman had just given me a nipple twister.

There was only one person I could possibly go with. And that was my best friend. Vanya.

The Big Question

When I walked into class on Wednesday morning, Vanya was sitting on her own. Jason was nowhere to be seen. This was the perfect opportunity. I was feeling quite nervous as I walked towards her. OK, I wasn't asking her to be my *girlfriend*. I don't want a girlfriend. I just needed a friend who was a girl to go with me to this prom. But still, what if she said no? What if she'd already agreed to go with someone else?

Only one thing for it.

I cleared my throat. 'Ahem! Vanya.'

Unfortunately, at the exact same moment, Jason Grooves swooped in front of me like a big, awful crow. The camera crew were behind him.

'That cough sounds nasty, Roman,' Jason said. 'You should hit my website. I'm selling Jason Grooves cough sweets on there now.'

I opened and closed my mouth a few times as he and Vanya did their stupid special handshake. This was terrible. How could I ask my big question with him here? Then it got worse.

'How grunk was last night, V-Unit?'

'Grunk?' I asked, a sour taste in my mouth. '*Last night?*'

Jason didn't even look at me to answer. 'Grunk. It's our new word instead of snife. We came up with it together last night.'

'Last night?' I said again.

'You'll never guess,' said Vanya, her cheeks flushed and her voice going at ninety miles an hour. 'So I was at home playing on my tablet and then I heard this noise from outside. And I looked out of the window and there's a HELICOPTER landing in my garden.'

I felt my stomach sink. 'A helicopter?'

Jason smiled. 'It was me.'

'Who else could it be?' I said, my mouth drier than a camel's trousers.

Jason didn't seem to hear me. 'Remember Monday. The V-Machine said she wanted to ride in Simon Bowel's helicopter. So I went and picked her and her whole family up in it last night. Bam!'

He did this wrist-flick finger-click thing to emphasise his point. Vanya copied him.

'Bam!' she repeated.

She was turning into him!

'Lovely,' I croaked.

'It was Simon Bowel's idea,' said Jason. 'He said we needed to spice up the TV show.'

'It was so grunk!' gushed Vanya, bouncing around her seat. 'We flew around for ages, looking down at all the buildings, then we landed in the park and Jason did a private concert just for us . . .'

'Sounds incredible,' I said flatly.

'Oh, you'd have loved it,' said Vanya. 'I asked Jason if we could pick you up on the way, but there wasn't space.'

'With the extra weight, we might not have got off the ground,' smiled Jason.

Charming. We stood there in silence for a few moments.

'Did you want to ask me something, Roman?' asked Vanya.

Helicopter rides. New words. The whole room felt like it was spinning. I heard myself say, 'I think I need to sit down.'

A Boost

So there I was. On my own. The better 50 per cent of my friends was turning into Jason Grooves. The other 50 per cent was visiting a school for naughty kids and I might never see him again after this week.

This was not grunk at all. Or broof. Or snife. Or even good.

I needed a boost.

And, amazingly, for the first time in ages, I got exactly what I wanted.

After Mrs McDonald had done the register, she asked me to take it back to the office. And it was when I got there that something truly magical happened.

There was nobody there, so I put the register down on the desk. Then I saw it: just a simple piece of paper with a few simple words on it. Even now, I can barely write it down because it makes a little tear of happiness come to my eye. It was a menu. A beautiful, gorgeous menu. It read:

YEAR SIX RANDOM MENU WEEK
WEDNESDAY

MAIN
SAUSAGE, BAKED BEAN, CHEESE AND JAM DOUGHNUT

DESSERT
JAM DOUGHNUT

My menu suggestion had been chosen! We were going to have DOUBLE DOUGHNUT for lunch.

'Sweet, succulent doughnuts,' I whispered.

The cook must've left it there for the lady who works in the office. For a moment I did nothing. I'm so used to things going badly for me that I didn't know how to react.

But then a tingly, fuzzy feeling of happiness and excitement built up in my stomach. It spread across my chest and tummy and down through my arms and legs.

'YAHHHHOOOOOOOOO!!!!!' I screamed.

'Is everything all right?' asked the office lady, as she came back in through the door.

'You betcha, sweet cheeks!' I cried.

She looked at me like I was completely nuts, but I didn't care. I danced – yes *danced* – out of the office and back towards the classroom.

Double doughnut for school lunch!

All those years of crummy, awful lunches. All those terrible things that had happened to me. All the rubbish with Jason and Vanya and Gamble and the TV show and the prom this week. None of it mattered now.

I clicked my heels and skipped across the library. I cartwheeled down the corridor. I even played the bongos on a Foundation Stage kid's head as I walked past her.

This was amazing. The greatest thing that'd ever happened to anyone ever. I felt alive. I felt powerful. I'd asked for the double doughnut and now I was going to get it. Nothing could stop me. I'd bounce right into that classroom. Ha ha! I'd even kiss Mrs McDonald on the lips.

And then, I thought, then I'd ask Vanya to come to the prom with me, and she would say yes and Jason Grooves could just go and eat his own pants because I had the power of the double doughnut and I could do ANYTHING!

I flung open the classroom door, ready to conquer the world.

Which is exactly when it all started to go wrong again.

Remember. This *is* my life we're talking about, after all.

A Change of Plans

Since I'd been out of the classroom, Trevor had appeared. He was standing at the front, with a laptop under his arm, face to face with Mrs McDonald. She was looking really angry with him for some reason.

'But you can't just keep changing everything,' she said, banging her hand against the table. 'First the prom. Now *all of this*.'

Trevor rolled his eyes. 'Look. I'm not saying we *can't* have the rounders match. Just not today, that's all.'

'But why?' said Mrs McDonald. Normally teachers don't have arguments in front of kids, but she was really fuming. It made me feel a bit uneasy. My warm fuzzy feeling was rapidly seeping away. 'The children have been looking forward to it.'

'Because I told you,' he replied. 'Rules two and six of a great TV series: keep it exciting and build up to the finale. It'll be better tomorrow afternoon. And we can do the leavers' assembly tomorrow morning.'

Mrs McDonald put her hands on her hips. 'And how are we supposed to prepare for the leavers' assembly if it's tomorrow? It's meant to be on Friday. We *were* going to practise all day tomorrow.'

Trevor waved his hand at her. 'Don't worry about practising. Jason's going to sing.'

Everyone went *yesssssss*.

Jason Grooves drabbed the class. 'JG is ripped and ready for action.'

For a moment, Mrs McDonald looked around, gasping for breath. 'I'll let him do *one* song and that's it. But you still haven't said *why* you're changing everything.'

Trevor sighed. 'Because we're giving the school money, so you need to do as I say. Got it?'

Mrs McDonald stood there with her mouth hanging open. The whole class went *ooooohhh*.

'Right,' continued Trevor, turning to face the class, 'who wants to watch the first episode of this TV show you've all been starring in?'

Everyone cheered.

Apart from me, that is. I was looking at Mrs McDonald. Her face was red, and tears were welling up in the corners of her eyes. I felt really sorry for her. At the start of the week she'd been so excited by the TV show. But now Trevor was trampling all over her like an evil goose.

Trevor didn't seem to care how nasty he was being. He whistled happily as he plugged his laptop into the interactive whiteboard. Someone turned out the lights. The following words appeared on the screen:

Jason: Grooving On as Normal
Episode One
Preview

Then my life suddenly got a lot, lot worse.

I won't describe everything that happened in the ten minutes of the TV show that we watched. I've already written about a lot of it. But I will tell you about *how* it had all been put together.

Almost everything had been fiddled around with to make Jason Grooves seem good. Like when he rescued Miss Clegg from the pool: it looked way more dramatic than it actually was. It was all in slow motion, with crashing music in the background and lots of close-ups of Jason looking brave. Then when Jason sang to Gamble, there was a long scene of everyone applauding and cheering and drabbing afterwards, even though that didn't really happen in real life. And after every scene, Jason would appear onscreen to say things like: 'I wouldn't call myself a hero – just an ordinary kid who happened to save a gigantic woman's life,' or 'I'm so glad my fans love my music as much as I love my fans.'

Yuck.

But these weren't the worst things about the TV show.

Basically, apart from the occasional scene with

the whole class in it, there were only three people in the whole episode.

The first two were Jason and Vanya.

Whenever Jason did something, the camera would cut to Vanya smiling, or looking impressed, even if she hadn't reacted like that at the time at all.

But the worst thing was that the third main person in the TV show was me.

Me.

Roman J. Garstang.

At first I couldn't figure out why I was getting so much screen time. I'm not exactly what you'd call interesting. There are bits of old carpet that are more exciting than me. Sometimes I even make myself feel bored. Why *did* they keep showing me on there?

It was only after a while that I started to realise.

And when I did, I felt my legs going weak and wobbly. A horrible, gurgling feeling grew in my stomach, and I had to grip the back of a chair to stop myself from falling over.

I was the villain.

This was terrible.

Every time I appeared, there'd be this creepy music, like when an evil doll comes to life in a horror film. And it only ever showed me looking jealous, or angry, or fed up. It was like the TV show was trying to make me out to be a monster.

There was one point when Jason said to the camera: 'I don't know why that kid Roman is trying so hard to be horrible. I forgave him for how he ruined the final of *BRT* for me. I just want to be his friend.' Then he kind of burst into tears, like I'd really upset him.

Even worse, they kept showing bits of the interview I did with Trevor yesterday. But they'd totally mucked about with it.

Remember, he asked me a load of silly questions to get me warmed up, then, afterwards, he'd asked all the proper ones? Well, on the TV show, they'd mixed up my answers to the questions, so it made it sound like I was a really nasty person. It went like this:

Question	What I actually said in real life	What I said on the TV show (taken from my answer to a different question)
Do you like Jason?	Yeah. He's all right.	Urgh. Gross. Stinks of wee.
Do you want Jason to be successful and famous?	That'd be good, I guess.	I'd rather eat slug brains. Imagine having to look at that giant fish head every day. Gross.
How does it make you feel when Jason sings?	Dunno. He's really good.	Makes me feel like Kevin *Vomasaurus Retch* Harrison riding on a roller coaster while trying to eat a yoghurt
How would you feel if someone went to the prom with your best friend?	Er . . . what? Sorry. I don't understand the question.	That cute little rodent belongs to me, you massive ugly spud. Now hand her over or I'll turn you into chips.

Luckily, Rosie Taylor came to the rescue. And trust me, that's not a sentence I ever thought I would write.

After about ten minutes of the TV show, she stormed out of her place and ripped the cable out of the back of the laptop. The screen went blank and she stood there, hands on hips, veins throbbing in her forehead, glaring at Trevor.

'Why is that turd-tastic little mutant getting so much time in front of the camera?' she snarled, jabbing a finger towards me. 'I thought this was a show about me and Jason falling in love with each other, not a documentary about the ugliest freaks in the universe. *Hashtag*: my eyes are burning.'

'W-well,' Trevor spluttered, backing away. He'd never seen a full-blown toddler tantrum from Rosie before. The rest of us weren't quite so scared – we'd seen loads of them. Like that time when Mrs McDonald asked Rosie to work with me and she screamed so loudly that the class goldfish died in its tank.

'Don't *w-w-well* me,' snarled Rosie. 'Sort. It. Out!'

Then she flounced out of the room dramatically, pausing at the door to shout at Jason, 'You'll be my boyfriend, whether you like it or not.'

I'm not sure that's how it works . . . I thought Somebody switched the lights on. Everybody looked at Jason, then at Vanya, then at me, then at the doorway that Rosie had just stormed out of. Nobody dared to speak.

'Maybe we should do some colouring in . . . ?' suggested Mrs McDonald, after what seemed like ages.

'I've got somewhere to be,' said Trevor, heading for the door. 'Jason. Five to twelve. Got it?'

Jason clicked his fingers and pointed at him. 'Got it.'

I walked over towards Vanya's table. 'Hey,' I said, 'I don't know what happ–'

'Get lost, Roman!' she snapped, spinning round to face me.

'But . . . but . . .' I said.

I'd never seen Vanya this angry before. Her face was all crumpled up with frown lines. 'How could you say those things about Jason? And me as well?'

'It's the way they changed it . . .' I said, but my voice came out as a pathetic whine.

'Oh, don't give me that,' she tutted. '*Cute little rodent,* am I? *Belong to you,* do I? *Turn Jason into chips,* will you? Well, here's some news for you. You can find yourself a new friend. And to think

I was going to ask you to go to the prom with me. You're just a . . .'

At that point, she covered her eyes with her hand and started crying.

I felt awful.

But then something happened that made me feel even worse.

Jason put his arm around her. His *arm*. Around *her*. 'I think you should leave her alone,' he said to me, as the camerawoman filmed from across the room. Then he whispered into Vanya's ear, 'Don't worry. I've got something at lunchtime that'll cheer you up.'

As he said that, he gave me the tiniest, nastiest, cruellest little wink. The kind of wink a wasp might give you just after flying out of your jam butty, and just before stinging you in the eyeball.

I stumbled back to my chair, feeling like I'd been kicked in the guts.

Gamble Returns

We spent the rest of the morning colouring in beach pictures, which is typical end-of-term time-wasting stuff. It was raining outside, so we worked right through breaktime and up to lunch. There was one good thing and one bad thing that happened during the session.

Good thing: Vanya cheered up quite quickly. She stopped crying and soon looked happy again.

Bad thing: it was Jason who cheered her up. At first he sang at her. Then he made her laugh. Before long, they were sharing a colouring sheet and whispering to each other, their heads leaning close together. I pressed down so hard that my felt tip broke through my paper. Then I realised that the camerawoman was filming me looking angry. *Perfect*. They'd make me look terrible in episode two as well.

I was feeling completely down. The only thing that kept me going was the thought of double doughnut for lunch. And even then I was struggling to get excited. There was a horrible taste in my mouth from the TV show and my argument with Vanya.

I can't believe I'm about to write this, but I was actually happy to see Gamble walking into the classroom about half an hour before lunch. He was looking really pleased with himself and he had a great big smile on his face.

Oh, and he wasn't wearing any trousers.

'Hello, Darren,' said Mrs McDonald. 'How was your visit to the Sunshine Unit?'

Gamble grinned. 'It was well good, miss. Mr Gibbons said he hasn't decided if I'm gonna go there yet and he's coming into school again tomorrow, miss, so I'm gonna be a good boy, innit, and I'm gonna be really helpful, so I can go to the good-boy school and be with my best mate Roman forever.'

I actually found myself smiling at this. I mean, obviously he's completely mental but he's still my friend. And I didn't have many of them left.

'Very good,' said Mrs McDonald, 'but – *ahem* – where are your trousers, Darren?'

Gamble twanged the elastic of his filthy under-pants (which I'm pretty sure were the same ones he'd worn for swimming on Monday, not that I keep a record of Darren's pants). 'Well, miss, see, I've already started being a good, helpful boy, innit.'

At that moment, Miss Clegg waddled into the classroom, looking flustered and fed up. 'Yeah,' she said flatly, 'really helpful.'

'Ah, shut up, you old kangaroo's willy,' said Gamble. 'I fixed your car, didn't I?'

Miss Clegg scowled at him.

'I don't understand,' said Mrs McDonald, confused.

Miss Clegg huffed out her cheeks. 'Everything was going fine. The Sunshine Unit was brilliant – a really miserable place where Darren could be treated cruelly for the next five years.'

Mrs McDonald frowned at her but Miss Clegg continued. 'Darren had already set off a fire extinguisher *and* had three fights – including one against himself. So it all looked great. He was doomed. Then we were about to come back but my car wouldn't start. So I went back inside to see if Mr Gibbons could call a garage for me . . .'

'And by the time she got back, I'd fixed it. Fan belt was broken, see,' said Gamble. 'I tied up my trousers and used 'em in the engine. Car runs as good as new, innit.'

Mrs McDonald squinted at him. 'Oh, Darren. I didn't know that you could mend cars.'

'Neither did I,' said Miss Clegg icily. She seemed really annoyed for someone who'd just had her car fixed for free.

Gamble grinned. 'Cars are well easy. My uncle Terry taught me how to break into 'em and start 'em without a key. I figured the rest out myself.'

'You could be a mechanic when you're older, Darren,' smiled Mrs McDonald proudly.

'Or a car thief,' grunted Miss Clegg.

'Miss Clegg, please,' said Mrs McDonald.

Gamble shrugged. 'Mneh. She's probably right.'

'So what happened next?' asked Mrs McDonald, trying to ignore that bit.

Miss Clegg huffed out her cheeks. 'Well, Mr Gibbons came out and found that Darren had mended my car . . .'

'And,' said Gamble, interrupting her, 'he said that it was a proper helpful, clever thing I'd done and if I carry on like that, I definitely won't be going to the naughty-boy school next year.'

'Oh, good for you!' said Mrs McDonald.

'Yeah. Really good,' said Miss Clegg, flopping down on to the seat.

For the rest of the morning, Gamble continued to be really helpful. Well, helpful in a Darren Gamble kind of way. For instance, he sharpened all the colouring pencils in the classroom. But then he ruined this by using them to make a model of a hand-held torpedo launcher he'd seen on the top-secret army website.

I have to say it *was* pretty impressive. Using

some Lego, a couple of elastic bands and a spring, he'd created something that could shoot deadly pencils right the way across the room from behind the bookshelf in the corner. The downside was that I spent the next half an hour ducking them.

The only good thing about this was that it kept my mind off Jason and Vanya. Until five minutes before lunchtime, that is, when Jason suddenly stood up on his table and drabbed the class.

Apart from me, everyone drabbed him back.

He ran his fingers through his enormous hair. 'Yo-o yo-o yooooo', he sang, his voice going up to a note so high that only bats would've heard it. 'I told you yesterday I got an announcement to make. And it is B to the I to the G, my brethren.'

'*Gruuuuuunk*,' said everyone. Loudest of all was Vanya. I felt myself grinding my teeth together.

'So,' he continued, 'see you lunchtime. I gotta go get ready. Ai-eeee!'

With that, he did a handstand on his desk then flipped off it on to the floor and disappeared.

Unfortunately, I was concentrating on him so much that I didn't have time to see the pencil missile that Gamble had fired at me.

'YOW!' I cried, putting my hand up to my head. The pencil had broken the skin and was sticking out sideways.

'Soz, Roman!' grinned Gamble, poking his head up from behind the bookcase. 'You shoulda ducked, innit!'

I pulled the pencil out again with a little pop. When I dabbed my finger against my head I felt a tiny drip of blood.

From Miss Clegg's reaction, though, you'd have thought I'd had my head chopped off. Within seconds, she'd bundled over and was poking my cut with her big clumsy banana fingers. 'Oh – oh. Looks nasty.'

I didn't like the way she looked hopeful when she said this. 'I think it's all right,' I said. 'Just a little scratch.'

'Oh, you *say* that,' she sniffed, 'but your brain could fall out. You'll be dead within minutes. Let's call an ambulance.'

An ambulance? Was she crazy? It wasn't that bad. And anyway, I was having the worst day ever and I wasn't going to miss out on double doughnuts now.

Then I realised something. 'Hang on,' I said, 'are

you *trying* to get me to go to hospital, so Darren gets in more trouble?'

'How dare you?' said Miss Clegg, looking shocked. 'I'm doing what's right for you. And if Darren ends up getting arrested for murder, well, that's his own fault and, hey! Where are you going?'

I turned round at the door. 'Lunch,' I said, before storming straight off to the hall.

I wouldn't normally act like this towards a member of staff, but I'd had enough. First Vanya, and now this. Well, there was no way I wasn't going to eat my double doughnut after the morning I'd just had. I marched straight to the lunch hall to collect what was mine.

Double Doughnut

I should've known something was wrong the moment I got inside the dining room. I didn't though. Perhaps I was just trying to kid myself. All I had left in the world was the double doughnut. I didn't want to imagine that that could let me down as well.

All of the tables had expensive-looking tablecloths

and little vases of flowers on them, and the knives and forks were laid out for us. None of the normal dinner ladies were there either. They'd been replaced by posh waiters and waitresses in black shirts. Over in the corner, a snooty woman was playing a violin. It was more like a smart restaurant than our school hall.

The only thing that looked out of place was a big shiny silver cannon in the middle of the room. *What on earth was that doing there?*

Gamble came up behind me and burped wetly in my ear. 'This is well smart, innit!'

Normally we queue up, collect our food from the counter, then go and sit down. But today, a waiter led us to a table.

Almost as soon as I sat, a waitress placed a plate in front of me. On it were three delicious, gorgeous, succulent doughnuts. They were perfect. The cheese was just slightly brown and crispy on top of the sticky jam. The dough had that deep brown crunchy look to it. A tiny trickle of bean juice oozed out of the hole at the side.

My stomach growled. I opened my mouth and plunged my head towards the plate.

'NO!' snapped the waitress. 'Wait till you're told.'

'Eh? Why?' I said, the drool dripping out of my mouth.

'Special menu today,' she replied.

Of course!

They were making an effort because today was the day of the double doughnut! It all made perfect sense. To me, anyway.

Or maybe I was just trying to convince myself that nothing was wrong.

'BOOM!' yelled a voice from the middle of the room.

We all looked up. 'Oh, great,' I said.

Jason Grooves was standing by the silver cannon thing, dressed in a chef's hat and an apron. Trust him to take over the greatest moment in the history of the world. 'Yo,' he said, 'I told you I had a big announcement to make today.'

There was a long pause, during which I was hoping he was going to tell us he was leaving the school forever. Instead, all he said was, 'Enjoy your meal. Peace out.'

And that was it.

'Huh,' I said to Gamble, picking up my knife and fork and slicing into the delicious doughnut. 'That wasn't much of announcement. Of course I'm going to enjoy my m–'

But then I stopped in my tracks.

How can I describe what happened next? It was like going to the cinema to watch *Car Chase Action Spy 3* and finding yourself locked inside a screen showing *Sparkly Rainbow Unicorns and the Glittery Sandals of Happiness*.

I'd cut open my doughnut. And instead of the oozing loveliness of sausages and baked beans, something else dribbled out. Something so disgusting that my head almost fell off with horror.

My doughnut was stuffed with thousands and thousands of spaghetti shapes in a red sauce.

But that wasn't the worst of it. I picked one of the shapes up with my fork and stared at it.

It was shaped exactly like Jason Grooves's head.

'What the slapped bottom is this?' I asked. I'd rather have eaten doughnuts that had been stuffed with angry wasps and dipped in dog dirt than this.

'Those, my friend,' said Jason behind me, 'are Spaghetti Grooves.'

Spaghetti Grooves

Before I could reply, there was a massively loud bang. Everyone gasped as millions and millions of shiny pieces of paper erupted into the air from the cannon in the middle of the room and fluttered down to the ground.

What was happening?

Everyone was dancing about, trying to grab the bits of paper as they floated towards them.

'You like the glitter cannon!' exclaimed Jason, leaping up on to my table. 'We borrowed it for the prom, but we thought we should get some use out of it.'

A glitter cannon? But *why*?

Jason drabbed at the school. 'Today, my brethren, is the worldwide launch of my new food – tinned Spaghetti Grooves.'

'Spaghetti *what*?!' I asked.

But Jason didn't answer. Instead he started singing a (thankfully) short rap about Spaghetti Grooves.

It went:

'If you're desperate for your life to improve,
Then grab yourself a Spaghetti Groove.
If you wanna sing like me and learn my moves,
Then stuff your face with Spaghetti Grooves.
It don't matter if you're fat or if you're thin,

You can eat my face straight out of a tin.
They come in a sauce,
You can feed 'em to a horse,
They're . . . *uh uh* . . . Spaghetti Grooves. Ai-eeee!'

Then he lowered his voice.

'Available in all supermarkets from Monday.'

Everyone went utterly insane. Seriously. The dinner hall hadn't been this excited since that time Gamble poured his favourite energy drink – Electric Muscle Spasm – into the beef stew. People were dancing and leaping around. Gamble smashed his face into his doughnuts and the sauce was splattered all over him like blood round the mouth of a lion. Kevin *Vomasaurus Retch* Harrison was spewing into the glitter cannon with excitement.

What was the fuss about?

Jason had ruined – completely *ruined* – the greatest meal of all time. People shouldn't have been celebrating. They should've been crying. It should have been like a funeral in there.

I pushed some Spaghetti Grooves across my plate. The sauce was all gloopy and had formed a rubbery skin on the top. How could this happen? One minute I was expecting the greatest meal of all time. And now I was faced with hundreds of miniature Jasons staring back at me.

Was there any way that things could get worse?

Well. I'd soon find out. This is *my* life after all.

'Yo yo yo!' said Jason, silencing the room. 'So I've got one person to thank for all this. And that's Roman Garstang.'

Eh?! I looked up sharply.

The camerawoman was right on the other side of the table from me, her camera pointing at my face.

Jason continued, 'If he hadn't sneezed spaghetti hoops on me the other day, I never would've had this idea. So he should be the one to have the first bite.'

A few people cheered. Some even started chanting my name: '*Ro-man. Ro-man. Ro-man.*'

'Take a nice big forkful and tell us what you think,' grinned Trevor from behind the camerawoman.

I pushed my plate away. 'I'm not really hun–'

Trevor came closer and whispered in my ear. 'It won't look good on TV if you don't eat them.'

His voice was threatening and cold. Like a sharp icicle hanging from the ceiling above my head.

I gulped. 'But I don't want to . . .'

'You know rule eight of a good TV show?' he said, quietly enough that nobody else could hear. 'You need a villain. You saw in episode one that *you* are that villain, my friend. Now eat the Grooves or you're gonna seriously regret it when we put together episode two.'

I gulped. Trevor patted me on the shoulder, then backed away. The camerawoman moved closer.

I didn't have a choice. Taking a deep breath, I closed my eyes and scooped some up. Maybe this wouldn't be so bad. I mean, if I couldn't see Jason's face, maybe they wouldn't taste quite so awful.

Very slowly, I lifted the fork to my mouth and eased it inside.

And that's when things *really* took a turn for the worst.

Hot Sauce

At first I didn't notice anything strange. I chewed once. Twice. Three times.

In the background, Jason was talking. 'I even chose all the ingredients myself . . .'

Then the flavour started to build up. It was weird.

I was expecting a tomato sauce but it wasn't. It was . . . hot.

The heat built slowly in my mouth. Gently at first, but then warmer and warmer. My lips began to tingle. My tongue began to burn.

Trevor grinned his super-fake fixed grin. 'How do you like Jason's special hot 'n' spicy sauce?'

'Hot and spicy?' I said. 'You are kidding me.'

I HATE hot food. I'm a total wimp when it comes to eating it. It makes my whole head feel like it's about to explode. And this stuff was absolutely scorching.

I was in agony. My throat felt like the inside of a volcano. I grabbed the jug of water from the centre of the table and chugged the whole lot back.

'Are you OK?' asked Gamble, concerned. 'Your face is turning red.'

I looked at my reflection in the back of my spoon. Darren was right. I could literally see my face changing colour, and my lips were throbbing and swollen.

'It's the sauce,' I gasped. 'It's way too hot.'

'Hmm,' said Trevor, 'maybe we got the recipe wrong.'

Do you think so, genius? It felt like I'd swallowed a blowtorch.

'Can you breathe?' asked Gamble. 'Do you need me to cut a hole in your throat and put a straw down your windpipe?'

'No,' I croaked, rattling the empty jug and wheezing like a straining dog. 'Water. More water.'

Gamble pulled the jug out of my hand and jumped up on the table. 'I'll save you, Roman! I'm proper helpful, me.'

He took a run-up and dived off the table. Unfortunately, as he did so, he stamped on the edge of my plate with his massive boot. This caused it to flip up, catapulting the Spaghetti Grooves right into my face.

At this point I learned a very important lesson: if something tastes hot and spicy, you probably don't want it to go in your eyes.

I screamed. The heat was tremendous. Fireworks burst in my eyeballs. I couldn't see and it felt like my face was going to peel off.

'Oops,' said Gamble.

'Someone get me a first aider!' I heard Trevor cry. 'If this kid dies we'll never sell a single tin of Spaghetti Grooves.'

Thanks for your concern.

The Sicky Chair

It took about five minutes of washing out my eyes before I could see again. Even then, everything was a bit blurry and my eyes felt like glowing coals. My face was puffy and swollen, and had turned a funny shade of purple.

What on earth was in that sauce? Petrol? Gunpowder? I mean, I know I'm a wuss when it comes to spicy food but *wow!* They could use that stuff to burn a hole in concrete.

Even after my eyesight had come back, I still felt a bit shaky. I had to sit on the Sicky Chair outside the office and wait to be collected by my mum. There are several terrible things about the Sicky Chair:

- as you probably guessed from the name, it's the chair where you sit if you're sick. Kevin *Vomasaurus Retch* Harrison spends about three quarters of his life in it. There are all these crusty *stains* dried into the cushions and it stinks like a mixture of stale yoghurt and rotten vegetables.
- it's right in the corridor, so people are constantly walking past you. Mostly, they just stared and

pointed at my massive purple head. But, unfortunately, some of them stopped to chat to me.

The first person was Gamble. 'Oh, wow!' he said.
'I wish my face would swell up like that.'

'It's horrible,' I said, my lips stinging with every
word. 'I thought I was going blind.'

'Huh!' he said. 'Some people have all the luck.'

I rolled my eyes. I didn't feel very lucky.

'Can I do summat to help you?' he asked.

'Help me?'

'Yeah. I need to be helpful and kind, and then
that Mr Gibbons will let me go to proper good-boy
school with you next year, innit.'

'You could steal me a new head.'

Gamble sniffed. 'All right. I'll see what I can do.'

The worst thing was, I don't think he was
joking.

Gamble was still there when the next person
came along. It was Jason Grooves. He'd removed
the chef's outfit. Behind him, Trevor was standing
alongside the camerawoman and sound technician.
'Yo, man. Sorry about your head.'

I shrugged.

'We're definitely going to change the recipe. Can

you just read this piece of paper for the camera?'

I did as I was told. My eyes were half-closed and a bit watery, so I had to read it one word at a time. Unfortunately, this meant that I didn't quite understand the meaning of it until I'd finished reading the whole thing.

'I promise,' I read, 'not to sue Jason Grooves or anyone else for what just happened. It is my own fault that I rubbed the special hot and spicy sauce into my eyes and that my face swelled up to this grotesque size.'

'Well done,' beamed Trevor. 'We got that on camera.'

Jason drabbed me. 'To make it up to you, I'm gonna give you a private gig right now.'

'There really is no need,' I said.

It was too late. Someone handed him a guitar and he sang me this hideous song called 'I Miss Your Massive Cheeks'. It was awful. And, because I was being filmed and I didn't want to look like the total villain in episode two, I had to sit there smiling and clapping throughout the whole thing. The words were weird – all about empty cages and half-drunk water bottles and wheels that didn't turn any more.

It was only when he finished that I realised what the song was about.

'What d'you think, man?'

I tried to frown but my head hurt too much. 'Was that song all about a . . . *dead hamster?*'

Jason sucked his teeth. 'For real, yeah. My pet hamster, Jason Junior. Makes me sad just thinking about him.'

'I'm sorry to hear that he's dead,' I said, glancing at the camera and trying to look concerned, despite the pain.

'He's not really dead,' said Jason. 'But I'm imagining how sad I'd be if he was.'

'Oh,' I said. *A memorial song for a hamster that's still alive. Nothing odd about that.*

Trevor leaned in. 'We're trying to show everyone that Jason is a really great guy and he loves animals. You know, after what happened with the sheep in the *BRT* final.'

'Don't mention that stupid woolly freak in front of me, man,' said Jason tetchily.

There was a long pause. 'So . . .' I said eventually, 'why exactly *did* you sing a dead hamster song at me?'

Jason shrugged. 'I think it fits your situation perfectly.'

'But I'm still alive. And also . . . well . . . I'm not a hamster.'

'Sure,' sniffed Jason, starting to look a little bit cross. 'But you *have* got fat cheeks like a hamster. And you *could've* died.'

I tried to fake a smile for the camera. 'You're right. It fits perfectly.'

Jason didn't seem to notice my sarcasm. He turned straight to the camera. 'That tune was called "I Miss Your Massive Cheeks". Available now online and from all good music stores. Check it out.'

Then, without saying anything else, they were gone and I was alone again.

A Visitor

Back at home, Mum made me lie on the sofa then force-fed me tomato soup all afternoon. She said I needed to get my strength up so I was ready for the prom tomorrow night. I didn't bother to tell her that, now Vanya hated my guts, I wasn't planning on going any more.

By the way, I can't stand tomato soup. It's meant to be *good for you* but how can it be good for you when it's made out of tomatoes? Tomatoes are a *fruit*, for heaven's sake. Who eats flipping *fruit* to make them feel better? Seriously, I'd rather eat a barrel of liquidised donkey nipples than a tin of that gunge. Every time she went out of the room, I tipped a spoonful into the plant pot next to the sofa.

I felt so rubbish that not even a sausage, beans and cheese doughnut the size of Jupiter would've made me feel better.

My eyes were still stinging. The good half of my friends had left me for Jason Grooves, who had just tried to burn me alive. Very soon I was going to be made to look like an awful person on national TV. And to cap it all off, the one and only school meal I'd ever wanted to eat had been snatched away from me at the last minute.

I was seriously depressed.

I'd been sitting there feeling sorry for myself for about four hours when the doorbell rang. Mum answered it then came into the lounge. 'Visitor. This'll cheer you up.'

She was wrong about that. Standing in the doorway was none other than Rosie Taylor, the worst person who's ever existed. *Oh, great.* Just when I thought my day couldn't get any worse . . .

Mum left us to it. Looking around the room in disgust, Rosie reached into her handbag, pulled out a pair of those blue shoe-protectors you get at the swimming pool and put them on.

'What are you doing?' I asked her.

'These shoes are worth seven hundred pounds,' she said. 'I am not putting them anywhere near the disgusting carpets in this shabby little dump. I'd rather walk barefoot through a pool of cows' brains.'

'Charming,' I said.

'How are you feeling?'

I raised an eyebrow. Rosie never cares how I feel. 'Fine.'

'Never mind. Still – *I* think Spaghetti Grooves are AMAZING. I even got my dad to buy two hundred tins to sell at his shopping centre.'

'Why are you here?' I sighed.

Rosie pursed her little slug's bum mouth. 'Because, you brainless pig fart, I am warning you one last time. If you don't get your friend Vanya away from my future husband, I am going to hold you responsible.'

'What?' I spluttered.

At that moment, my mum walked back through

the room. She was wearing her scruffy gardening clothes.

Rosie instantly put on a big fake smile. 'Oh, by the way, Mrs Garstang. I love your outfit. It's gorgealumptious.'

'Such a sweet girl,' said Mum as she disappeared upstairs.

As soon as she'd gone, Rosie's face dropped. '*Urgh*. If you ever see *me* wearing minging rags like *that*, feel free to shoot me.'

'My pleasure,' I said.

'So anyway,' said Rosie, shaking back her hair. 'This TV show is my big chance of fame. I *need* to go to that prom with Jason Grooves. And if I don't, it'll all be your fault. You'll have ruined my life and I will not be responsible for what happens next. Got it?'

'Why would it be my fault?'

Rosie rolled her eyes. 'Because, you spectacular dimwit, *you* are best friends with that hideous melon-head Vanya Goyal. So *you* should be taking her to the prom. Jason wants me to go with him.'

'Then why hasn't he asked you already?'

'A lot of boys are frightened of my beauty,' said Rosie. 'He's probably worried that I'll say no because I'm too good looking for him. But I've already told him. If he invites me, I'll make myself five per cent less beautiful on the night, so I don't make him look bad.'

I really tried not to laugh here but it was impossible. I laughed so hard I thought the skin on my face would split open. Rosie is convinced she's gorgeous. In actual fact, she's got a face like an octopus's buttocks.

Rosie stared daggers at me and I stopped laughing immediately. 'Why don't you just ask him yourself?' I said.

'Wow. You are literally the stupidest person on the planet,' she said. 'I have honestly met bags of dog dirt hanging from trees with more brains than you.'

'Thanks a lot.'

'I'm a princess. And princesses do *not* do the asking.'

'I always thought boys and girls were equal.'

'Well, you're even thicker than you look.'

She came right over and grabbed my sensitive face with her sharp fake nails. The pain was excruciating – like that time Gamble poured ants down my undercrackers. 'I'm serious,' she growled. 'Don't let Vanya go to the prom with Jason, or you'll pay.'

Then she swept out of the room and was gone.

This was ridiculous. How on earth was I supposed to go to the prom with Vanya? She hated my guts. I wiggled my cheeks, poured the rest of my tomato soup into the plant pot and slumped back on to the sofa.

What a day.

Of course, for me, tomorrow can always be worse.

THURSDAY

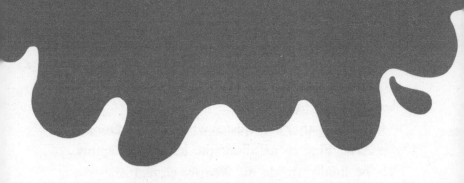

Morning

Gamble Is Helpful and I Show Off My Skills at Rounders

Unfortunately, my face was back to normal on Thursday morning and I had to go back to school. Vanya turned away as soon as I walked into the classroom. I huffed out my cheeks and slumped into the chair next to Gamble's empty space. He was nowhere to be seen.

'Done a runner, I'll bet,' said Miss Clegg to Mr Gibbons. 'He knows he can't trust himself in the leavers' assembly. Last year we did a class assembly about germs and he threw a handful of verrucas into the audience.'

'Hmm,' said Mr Gibbons, jotting something down.

I gulped. Today was Gamble's last chance to prove he was a good kid for Mr Gibbons. He really should've got here on time.

It was only after the register, when Mrs McDonald was explaining to us about the leavers' assembly, that he finally strode in. Weirdly enough, he was with Trevor the TV man. When they came through the door, Trevor patted him on the back and Gamble came over and sat down next to me.

'What was all that about?' I asked Gamble.

'Trevor's gonna help me today,' he whispered back.

'Really?' Trevor didn't seem to be the kind of person who helped anyone apart from himself.

'Yeah. I'm gonna be a good, helpful boy for him, then he's gonna give Mr Gibbons a proper good report about me and then I'll go to good-boy school with you, innit.'

I narrowed my eyes. 'What do you mean – a good, helpful boy for him?'

Gamble tapped his nose with a filthy finger. 'Can't tell anyone, innit. It's a surprise to make the TV show more exciting.'

I didn't like this. 'What's he asked you to do?'

Gamble grinned. 'Well. I've said I'll do one thing

for him, right, but then I've also done this other thing that he doesn't know about cos I thought two things are better than one and . . .'

Before he could finish, he was interrupted by Mrs McDonald. 'Good morning. As you know, we haven't had any time to prepare our leavers' assembly . . .' She pursed her lips and glanced at Trevor. 'So when it's your turn to speak in there, just stand up and say what your favourite memory of the school has been. It'll have to do.'

'Don't worry, Mrs McDumbledore,' said Trevor, 'we've got a plan to make it more exciting. Ain't that right, Jason?'

Jason cleared his throat and looked around him. It was the first time I'd ever seen him looking unconfident. 'T-Bone,' he said to Trevor, 'I've been thinking and maybe we ain't doing the right thing . . .'

Trevor spoke through gritted teeth, without moving his lips. 'Jason. Not here, in front of everybody. We've been through this a million times. You want this show to make it on to TV, don't you? You want to be famous?'

Jason looked around. Everyone was staring at him and wondering what was going on. 'It's just . . . that one's OK but . . .'

'Stick to the plan,' snapped Trevor, who really seemed to be getting cross now. 'Rules three, four, five and eight, remember?'

Jason took a deep breath. 'OK.'

'Are you OK, Jason?' asked Rosie Taylor. 'I mean, if you need me to kiss anything better, you only have to ask. And by the way there are only a few hours till the prom and you haven't got a date yet so I can always . . .'

Jason looked at the floor.

'It's all under control,' Trevor said to Rosie.

Rosie pursed her slug's bum mouth and strutted back to her seat. 'He'd better not ask Vanya or you're dead,' she hissed at me.

Me? I thought. Geez. I didn't know what I was supposed to do. Vanya wasn't even talking to me, so I didn't know how I was supposed to take her to the prom.

Actually, I wasn't fussed about what Rosie had said – she threatens to kill me at least six times a day. No, I was more interested in two other things:

- **What exactly was Gamble going to do to help Trevor?** He said he'd agreed to do one thing to help him, and he'd come up with another favour as a surprise. This wasn't good. Gamble's surprises normally involve something painful or disgusting or both. Like that time when he brought all his old baby teeth into school and hid them in my cheese butty.

– **What was Trevor on about to Jason?** *Rules three, four, five and eight?* Now what *were* they? Hmm . . . *have a love interest . . . you've got to like the main character* . . . err . . . *rivalry and competition.*

And the last one was . . . oh no. My skin turned cold.

Rule eight: *you need a good villain.*

I already knew that the villain was me. But what were they going to do to me?

I suddenly felt very worried about the leavers' assembly.

Leavers' Assembly

Normally, the leavers' assembly is a big show-stopping thing with songs, speeches, funny sketches and cute photos from when the Year Sixes were little. Because the TV show had taken up the whole week and given us hardly any time to prepare, this one was a lot less exciting.

Well, until the end anyway.

The whole school was crammed into the hall, with all the parents on chairs at the back. My mum was in the front row of the chairs, loudly crying her eyes out and wailing that her little baby boy was all grown up, which was totally embarrassing. Gamble's mum and dad hadn't turned up. Apparently, his big brother Spud was in hospital after eating a tablet last night.

'Oh no!' I said to him as we sat down. 'That's really bad. You shouldn't eat medicine if it's not meant for you.'

'Medicine?' Gamble asked, looking at me funny. 'No! Not that kind of tablet! I mean, he bit a chunk out of his iPad cos it wouldn't work after it fell down the bog.'

'Oh,' I said. The entire family is nuts.

Anyway, the assembly was pretty lame. We were on benches at the front, and we all had to stand up and take turns to speak into a microphone. My favourite memory was when I almost got to eat a double doughnut (I didn't mention that it was shortly followed by my least favourite memory). Gamble's was the day he set fire to Miss Clegg while she napped in class (you can imagine how fast Mr Gibbons was writing on his clipboard when he said *this*). Rosie had two favourite moments – the day Jason returned to school and that time when I fell down the stairs in Year Two. Kevin *Vomasaurus Retch* Harrison said his best memory was when he got out of cross country by drinking three litres of banana milkshake and spewing into his PE bag.

Then it was Jason's turn. For some reason I didn't like or understand, Trevor had insisted on Jason sitting next to me. Of course, Jason didn't use the same microphone as everybody else. He had one of those special, professional ones with a little earpiece and a tiny straw thing that sticks to the side of your cheek. He always used one on *BRT* so he could dance and sing at the same time.

Still looking nervous, he stood up. It was really weird – it wasn't like him to lack confidence at all. The camerawoman was filming him from the side. He cleared his throat and looked over at Trevor.

'I ain't sure . . .' he croaked.

There were a few mutters in the audience. Some of the mums went *aaaaawwwww*.

In front of everybody, Trevor strode over and

spoke to him in a low voice. Even right next to them, I could only hear the odd word: '. . . just follow the plan . . . do as you're told . . . want to be famous, don't you?'

It was clear that Trevor was losing patience with him.

What was *going on?*

'OK,' said Jason, taking a deep breath. He slapped himself in the face and wiggled his massive hair. It seemed to give him new belief in himself. 'Yo yo yo!' he said, drabbing the audience.

They all drabbed back.

He swallowed. 'Turns out my best moment ain't happened yet.'

Everyone went *oooohh*. The camerawoman stepped closer.

'Now y'all know I ain't chosen my date for tonight. I wanted to leave it till the last minute.'

Ooooh, said everyone again.

He looked over at Trevor, who gave him the thumbs up and mouthed: *perfect*.

I didn't like this at all.

Jason swallowed hard. 'So I got a tough choice to make between two beautiful girls. Stand up, Vanya and Rosie.'

There were two things wrong with what he'd just said. First of all I didn't want him going to the prom with Vanya, even if she hated me. And secondly, Rosie? *Beautiful? ?* It's not nice to say it, but she looks like a terrified emu.

Vanya stood up nervously, but Rosie leapt to her feet, quickly slathering lipstick on to her face. By the way, people aren't meant to have make-up in school but last year Rosie got a letter from her doctor (which she clearly wrote herself) saying that, if she couldn't wear make-up at all times, she would 'literally die of embarrassment' and 'her blood would be on Mrs McDonald's hands'.

'So,' Jason said, his voice still shaking. 'One of you girls is gonna be my date tonight. The other is gonna miss out. I can reveal that the girl who's going to the prom with me is . . .'

Everything seemed to slow down.

There was a long pause, just like when they announce the winners on *BRT*. Someone dimmed the lights. The whole audience began a drumroll on their knees. I glanced over at Vanya. I couldn't read her face – was she excited? Nervous? A little freaked out? Meanwhile Rosie was practically having an asthma attack. 'OMG-OMG-OMG-OMG-OMG-

OMG!' she squealed, crossing her fingers and bouncing up and down like a mad kangaroo.

I realised that Trevor had produced a second camera, which he was pointing directly at me. I was just wondering why, when Jason closed his eyes, then slowly said, 'Vanya!'

I opened my mouth but no sound came out. All around the room people were cheering and cooing and whooping and drabbing. Rosie screamed, then staggered off out of the room, ranting that 'someone would pay for this'.

'Excellent,' said Trevor from the side of the room.

The crowd quietened down. They were all staring at Vanya now. The camerawoman was so close that she probably could've counted Vanya's eyelashes.

'Oh,' said Vanya, looking uncomfortable. 'Well . . . I mean . . . er . . . I *like* you and we're good friends, but er . . . I've been thinking . . .'

My eyebrows shot up my forehead. It sounded as if . . . surely not . . . but maybe . . . *was she about to turn him down?*

This was great!

Over at the side of the room, Trevor looked like he was going to explode.

Vanya glanced down at me – *ME*, I might just say here – then continued. 'I'm not sure because . . .'

But before she could finish, there was a blood-curdling scream from outside the hall.

Kick Its Head In

Everyone spun round. Moments later, the door flew open, and there was Rosie, lipstick smeared across her face. 'Help!' she cried. 'It's a . . .'

She didn't get the chance to finish. But she didn't need to either because, at that moment, something smashed into her from behind and knocked her to the floor.

There was total chaos in the hall.

The people closest to the door were scrambling out of the way. Children in the front few rows were screaming. Teachers were panicking and flapping their arms about.

Then I saw why.

A *sheep*.

There was a flipping sheep in our leavers' assembly. A big male one, with horns and wool and legs and everything. It charged past our class and into the audience, bucking and tossing its head about as kids clambered over each other to escape.

What the stuffed doughnut was going on here?

'Go on, Jason! Kick its head in!' screamed Gamble.

Jason didn't answer him. He was dealing with the situation bravely. Well, by 'bravely' I mean he'd run away and was now halfway up the wall bars, wailing like a baby.

Gamble looked at him, then huffed out his cheeks. 'All right. Fine,' he sighed. Then he strode into the audience, his arm raised above his head. I noticed a pointy silver thing in his hand. With a swipe of his arm, he plunged it into the sheep's neck. The sheep wobbled around for a few moments. Then it slumped to the ground and was still.

The whole hall went quiet, apart from the snoring of the sheep and the sound of Jason weeping from high above us.

'Oh, this is marvellous!' Trevor said, focusing his camera on him. 'Keep those tears flowing, Jason. This'll look great on TV.'

Who Was Responsible?

After the assembly was cut short and the hall evac-
uated, we all went back to class. Jason Grooves
was sitting on a chair, a blanket wrapped around
his shoulders. He was drinking a hot cup of tea
that Trevor had brought for him, and making these
strange whimpering noises.

Oh, please, I thought. It was a sheep, not a
flipping T-rex.

And do you want to know the worst thing?
Vanya had her arm around him. Her arm!
Everything had looked great for a few seconds in
the assembly – like she might reject him or something. **And now she was hugging him!** This was a
disaster.

'Say something, Jason,' urged Trevor.

'But I don't feel li–'

'Do it!' said Trevor.

Jason sighed. He squeezed Vanya's hand and
gazed into her eyes like he was a sick puppy or
something. 'I don't think I could take any more
bad news today.'

What a weasel!

'Oh – er . . . well . . .' said Vanya.

I gulped. Was she about to agree to go to the prom with him?

Luckily, Mrs McDonald interrupted her.

'Right,' she said, from the front of the room. 'Who was responsible for bringing a sheep into our leavers' assembly?'

Of course, we all knew the answer to this already. Everyone turned towards Gamble. In the corner, Mr Gibbons' pencil whizzed across his clipboard.

'I was trying to be nice to Jason, innit,' protested Gamble. 'He said he hated sheep. I nicked it off a farmer. I thought me and him could take it out at playtime and take turns punching it. It was meant to stay in the toilets till then.'

'But Jason loves all animals,' said Trevor loudly. 'He does **not** hate sheep at all. Remember that. Rule four – we've got to like the hero.'

Jason muttered something under his breath.

'Darren. You brought a stolen sheep into school so that you could . . . *beat it up?*' asked Mrs McDonald, removing her glasses.

Gamble looked confused. 'Yeah. It was meant to be a surprise. I thought Trevor and Jason would put in a good word for me with Mr Gibbons afterwards.'

Without looking up, Mr Gibbons turned over his page and kept on writing.

'I don't really understand . . .' said Mrs McDonald. She wasn't the only one.

'Jason kept saying he was upset after he lost to that juggling sheep in the *BRT* final,' said Gamble, 'so I thought it'd make him feel better if he could batter a sheep.'

If you ignored the fact that Gamble was going to attack a poor, defenceless animal which he'd kidnapped from a farm, I guess that this was actually quite a kind idea.

It was hard to ignore the bit about kidnapping and attacking the sheep though.

'Told you. The kid's completely crazy,' said Miss Clegg to Mr Gibbons.

'Hmmm,' replied Mr Gibbons, still writing. 'Very interesting.'

This was terrible. Not only was one of my best friends hugging Jason Grooves, but my other one was getting an even more awful report than before. He'd definitely be sent to the behaviour unit now. This day just got worse and worse.

I took a deep breath. *Someone* had to do something. *Someone* had to try and save Gamble from this total mess. And then maybe Vanya might think that this *someone* was a nice person who tried to help other people. And then she might stop hugging other people.

'It was my fault,' I said loudly. Everyone turned to face me now.

Was this such a good idea after all? Probably not, but it was too late – I had to keep going. 'I . . . er . . . told him to do it. Darren was innocent. If anyone gets into trouble, it should be me.'

The camerawoman pointed her camera at me.

'This could work,' said Trevor. 'Nice bit of drama with our evil villain.'

'But Darren said . . .' began Miss Clegg.

'He lied,' I said, swallowing hard. 'He was trying to save me. He always does stuff like that because he's a really great kid. I brought the sheep in. Lucky Darren was here to put it to sleep. He's a hero.'

'Why would you bring a sheep to school?' asked Mrs McDonald, totally confused.

Jason glared at me. 'Huh. Obvious. He wanted to upset me. Kid's been shredding my tangerine ever since I came back. And I've been trying to be friendly.'

Vanya was shaking her head and looking at me with total disgust.

This hadn't worked out quite as well as I'd hoped. Maybe sticking up for Gamble wasn't such a great idea after all.

'Is this true, Darren?' asked Mrs McDonald.

Gamble looked at Mr Gibbons, then at Jason, then at me. *At least I can still help Gamble*, I thought. Reluctantly, I gave him a little nod. He seemed to understand and he sniffed. 'Yep. Lucky I always carry a tranquilliser dart just in case.'

There was a long pause.

'I'm sorry. Just in case of *what*?' asked Mrs McDonald.

'Dunno.' Gamble shrugged. 'I might need to knock someone out so I can pull out their teeth without them noticing or summat. I mixed the poison myself.'

Mrs McDonald pretended not to hear him. 'And what are we going to do with a sleeping sheep? It's still in the hall.'

'Make burgers out of it?' suggested Gamble.

A couple of people gasped in horror. Mr Gibbons was writing so fast his hand was a blur.

'All right, all right,' Gamble said. 'Call my uncle Terry. He'll come and get it in his van.'

'And hurry up about it,' snapped Trevor. 'We've

got to start setting up the hall for the prom right away.'

Mrs McDonald sighed. 'Roman. Can you please say sorry to Jason?'

She sounded like she knew it wasn't really me who was responsible for the sheep.

I mumbled an apology to Jason without looking at him.

Mr Gibbons seemed to be rubbing out everything he'd just written.

'Oi! McDonald,' said Miss Clegg, 'you can't seriously believe it was Roman. It must've been Darren. The kid's a nutter. He's always doing stuff like this. Remember when we had those baby chicks in class and he tried to swallow one whole?'

Mrs McDonald ignored her. 'Miss Clegg. Please could you ask the caretaker to move the sheep out of the hall, then call Darren's uncle?'

Miss Clegg let out a massive sigh, like she'd just been asked to unblock a toilet with her bare hands or something. 'Of course, Your Majesty,' she muttered as she left the room. 'What did your last slave die of?'

Boring Morning

The rest of the morning was pretty boring. We had to make a pile of all our old school books to take home. My punishment for the sheep was to do this in the corridor away from everyone else. I didn't mind too much. It meant I didn't have to be in the same room as Jason, Trevor, Vanya, Gamble or Rosie.

Because Gamble was being interviewed by Mr Gibbons somewhere, I had to sort out his books as well. He'd done hardly any work all year. His maths book had a massive bite out of the corner and his English book looked and smelled like he'd eaten fish and chips off it. Tucked into his Romans topic folder was a flattened dead frog. And the only piece of work in his geography book was a map of the world, with all of the countries coloured in black. It had the title: 'Wot wil bee left wen I mayk my bomb.'

All morning, I kept my eye on Jason through the classroom window in the corridor. Because he had no work to sort out, he just spent the whole time chatting to Vanya.

I kept on thinking about when he'd asked her

to the prom. It had *sounded* like she was about to say no. But then again, she'd been so friendly with him all week that I didn't know what to think. It was really confusing and made my brain hurt.

The strange thing was that Jason kept looking across the room as Vanya was talking to him. It was like he was more interested in something else. I couldn't quite tell who or what he was looking at, but a few times Trevor stopped the filming and told him off.

At lunchtime, Trevor had organised a load of workmen to come in and sort the hall out for the prom. We had to eat in the classroom.

Because of this, the Year Six Random Choice Menu had been completely cancelled. The food was absolutely horrific: leftover spaghetti hoops from the other day. Obviously, I didn't eat any of these. It meant that all I could have on my plate were a couple of 'Potato Groofles'. These were another new Jason Grooves product – this time potato waffles in the shape of Jason doing the drab.

Surprisingly enough, I didn't fancy eating them either, so I was absolutely starving by the time the afternoon came around.

During the rest of lunchtime, everyone signed

each other's shirts. People weren't really talking to me after they'd seen episode one of the TV show, so the only person who signed mine was Gamble. Well, I say 'signed'. Actually he just drew an enormous pair of boobs right across the front of it.

Rounders

In the afternoon, I was allowed back in class for the big rounders match that Mrs McDonald had been banging on about all week. Of course, I didn't really want to play. I hate rounders. It's totally pointless. Someone throws a ball. Someone else hits it with a stick. They run round in a circle while other people try to tap the ball against some posts. The end.

See: rubbish.

And it doesn't help that I'm about as good at hitting the ball as a drunk jellyfish holding a piece of celery in its bottom.

Last term in PE we all had to invent our own sport. Mine was called Doughnutball. It's way better than rounders and much easier to play. Basically, you split into two teams, sit down on the grass and eat doughnuts all afternoon. We weren't allowed to play this though. Apparently, it wasn't 'healthy enough' and PE is about 'being active' and 'keeping fit'.

We all went out on to the field. Trevor split us into two teams (Mrs McDonald seemed to have given up on being in charge, and Trevor said he wanted to 'get the balance right' for the TV show).

This meant that I was on a team with Rosie Taylor, while Vanya and Jason were on the other team. I was a bit cheesed off about this – the last time I was on Rosie's team for rounders, she accidentally hit me with her bat. Well, I say 'accidentally' – she did chase me round the field three times first.

'The Groove-stars will bat second,' said Trevor.

'We usually toss a coin,' replied Mrs McDonald.

Trevor ground his teeth together. 'We're making a TV show. I don't care. Bald man. Will you keep score? You've got a clipboard.'

Mr Gibbons looked up from where he was standing at the side of the pitch. 'Oh no. Sorry. I'm just here to watch young Darren. And . . . er . . . speaking of Darren. What's he doing over there?'

Gamble was at the far side of the field, scrambling over the fence from the staff car park. Weirdly, he seemed to be coming from the TV crew's van. When he reached the field, Trevor the TV guy winked at him. Gamble winked back.

This was seriously weird.

'What's going on?' I whispered to Gamble, as he lined up next to me.

Gamble tapped his nose. 'Top secret, innit. Told you – I'm trying to show what a helpful kid I am.'

I don't like it when Gamble is secretive. Like that time he entered me for the 'Miss Bikini Babe Worldwide' beauty competition by sending in Photoshopped pictures of my head stuck on to the body of a woman in a swimsuit. I only found out when I got invited to America to take part in the final.

As he sat there, ignoring me, the game started.

Here are the highlights:

There were no highlights.

My team scored six rounders, but I didn't really help much with this. On my turn, I managed to hit the ball, which was a completely new experience for me. Unfortunately it went straight up in the air, bounced off the top of my head and was caught easily by Jason Grooves at backstop. He celebrated by triple backflipping over to Vanya, then doing this stupid dance with her. I nearly cried.

On Gamble's turn, he managed to score a rounder without actually hitting the ball. When it was bowled to him, he caught it, shoved it down his undies, then ran all the way round. Nobody tried to stop him.

'Shouldn't he be out?' asked Trevor.

Mrs McDonald shook her head. 'We don't

normally say that Darren is out. There was an . . . *incident* last year. One of the other children had to have a rounders post removed from his nose.'

'Oh,' said Trevor.

After that, we got a fresh ball (nobody was going to touch the one that'd been down Gamble's pants without a pair of thick gloves) and my team had to field.

Nothing interesting happened until the last batter came forward, with the scores tied at six rounders each. It was then that everything went very, very wrong.

A Slap in the Ear

Of course, Trevor had arranged it so that Jason could hit the winning rounder. Jason swaggered up, swinging the bat around and spinning it over his wrists.

'OK,' said Mrs McDonald, with the camera pointing at her. 'Score this rounder and your team wins, Jason.'

The camera and everyone else's eyes turned towards Jason. Off the pitch, Vanya Goyal was cheering him and clapping her hands.

Suddenly, I had this burning feeling that took over my whole brain. I *had* to stop him scoring the winning run. This was totally unlike me. Normally I couldn't care less about winning or losing in rounders. Usually the only thing I worry about is making sure I don't get caught eating the secret doughnut I smuggle on to the pitch under my T-shirt.

But not today.

As Jason took up his position, I suddenly felt something I'd never felt before: *I wanted to do well in PE*. I wanted to get him out. I wanted to stop him from winning. He'd messed up this whole week with this TV show, and the prom, and making Vanya hate me. And now I wanted to do something about it.

'I'm warning y'all. JG does not like to lose at anything,' he said.

The ball was lobbed towards him and he pulled back his bat. I crouched forward, ready to spring into action to stop the ball when he hit it.

Then something really surprising happened.

He missed.

It was a terrible miss as well – a massive, dramatic air-shot that caused his whole body to spin round three times.

It turned out that Jason was absolutely RUBBISH at rounders. Even worse than me. It took him about nine goes just to hit the ball. And every time he missed it, Trevor would shout, 'CUT! That one didn't count. Too high.' Or 'Too low'.

It was all getting a bit embarrassing. Even most of *my* team wanted him to hit the winning rounder so we could all go back inside. Apart from me though. I was not going to let him win.

Eventually, and after some serious coaching by Vanya, he finally managed to hit the ball. It looped high into the air. Up. Up. Up.

Cheered on by his team, Jason set off running.

Past first base.

The ball slowly began to arc downwards. I fixed my eyes on it and ran sideways left. Then right.

Round second base.

The ball was coming straight at me now.

Dodging outside third base.

'Yours, Roman!' someone yelled.

The world slowed down. Time turned to syrup.

Closing in on fourth.

The ball almost hovered down towards my outstretched hands.

'NOOOOOO!' shouted Trevor.

It landed in my palms and I closed my fingers around it. I'd caught i—

'Ooooof!' I cried, as something smashed into my back.

The ball flew out of my hands.

I slammed face first into the ground.

When I looked up, Jason was being filmed prancing past fourth base. His team were drabbing like maniacs.

But who . . .

'Soz, mate,' said Gamble, his body tangled up with mine.

'What did you do that for?' I groaned. I felt like I'd just been pushed through a car crusher. 'We're on the same team.'

'Gotta look like a helpful kid for Mr Gibbons, innit,' he said.

I sat up painfully. To the side of the pitch, Jason was being thrown into the air by his team while the camerawoman filmed him.

'Now!' cried Trevor, turning round to face me and Gamble, and waving his mobile in the air.

'What's he on about?' I asked.

Gamble sniffed. 'And I'm sorry for this too, Roman.'

'Sorry for wh–'

There was a sudden slap across my ear. My hearing went all weird and stuffy. I felt dazed and confused. I tried to lift my hand to my ear, but Gamble was pinning me down.

'Done it!' he called.

Then something just kind of went *click* inside my brain.

Everything suddenly felt miles away: the voices shouting at me, the other people on the field, the whole rest of the world.

I felt like I was being sucked into a black hole.

My surroundings melted away.

There may have been some cheering.

I think I saw Trevor messing about with his phone.

Maybe Jason's teammates had put him down or maybe he'd somersaulted off their shoulders.

I wasn't paying attention.

Because only one thing mattered now.

Jason.

He was like a single candle in the centre of a dark cave. A solitary Jelly Tot on a cake. The last doughnut in the box.

There was nothing else in the world apart from him.

It was all suddenly crystal clear to me.

I had to hurt Jason Grooves.

I marched forward, like a robot, or a puppet, or a zombie. I didn't know *why* I had to hurt him. I didn't question it at all. I just carried on, my eyes locked on to him, my arms stretched out in front of me. Cold rage surged through my body.

Jason had to be eliminated.

Closer and closer.

Past Trevor, who was watching me and still fiddling with his phone.

Jason was in front of me now, his back turned to me, dancing and singing with his teammates. It was like I was watching myself on TV. I saw my hands rise towards the back of his head, like they were being pulled up by invisible strings.

He turned. Noticed me. Saw my hands as they closed round his neck. Screamed in horror. And then . . .

THUD!

Vanya punched me in the side of the head and I fell to the ground.

The Worst

I was sitting on the floor, dazed and confused. A crowd of people were surrounding Jason, who was looking terrified. Vanya was closest to him, holding his hand. 'Jason,' she said, 'I *will* go to the prom with you.'

Then she looked at me like I was a nit she'd just found in her breakfast.

'I . . . I . . .' I spluttered, but she'd already turned away. What on earth had come over me?

Jason rubbed his neck. 'Oh. That is . . . er . . .'

'Perfect!' announced Trevor, striding in front of me. 'Jason, perhaps you could give your date a kiss on the cheek for the camera . . .'

'We're not going to kiss,' she said.

'Just a teeny-weeny peck?' pleaded Trevor. 'It'll be great for the TV show.'

'I'm going to the prom with him because he's my best friend. Friends don't kiss,' she said, then she turned and glared right at me. 'And they don't attack people either.'

Jason was her best friend. And she hated me. I could've cried.

Just then, Rosie stormed up to Vanya and Jason.

'Nobody rejects Rosie Taylor. *Hashtag*: prepare to suffer.'

Trevor grinned. 'Nice bit of rivalry there. Rule five.'

Rosie stormed off across the field. Jason raised a finger and was about to speak but Trevor placed his hand on his shoulder. 'Maybe we could just film that bit again with you and Vanya. Try to look a little bit happier when she says she'll go with you.'

Jason sighed.

I looked around me. Mr Gibbons had reached down to the floor and picked something up. He turned it over in his hand a few times and examined it carefully. It was cone-shaped and about the size of a twenty-pence piece.

Gamble ran up, snatched it from his hand, and ran away across the field.

What on earth was going on?

Evening:
The Night of
the Prom

My Fairy Godmother Arrives and
I Go Out for a Kiss

Of course, I was sent home from school for attacking Jason, and banned from going to the prom. My mum couldn't believe it when she got the call. I'm the softest kid in Europe. Seriously, when I was ten I got beaten up by my three-year-old cousin (although in my defence she was armed with a cuddly Iggle Piggle toy. That soft blanket he carries can be deadly in the wrong hands). Having never told me off for fighting before, Mum didn't know what to do with me when we got home. All she could do was send me to my room.

It was obvious that this was all Gamble's fault – the cosy chats with Trevor, coming out of the TV van after lunch, the slap in the ear, the thing he snatched from Mr Gibbons' hand.

I was almost certain of what he'd done. It had been like I wasn't in control of my own actions; like someone else had taken over my brain. And to do that, they'd have needed a special machine – a brain controller. Just like the one from the army website that Darren had been on about all week.

Back in class, I'd tried to explain this to Vanya. She didn't believe me. She'd lowered her voice and whispered that I'd *gone too far this time* and she *never wanted to see me again.*

'But . . . but . . .' I'd said.

Vanya had narrowed her eyes. 'Do you know why I didn't say yes when Jason asked me to go to the prom with him in assembly?'

I shook my head.

'I realised I wanted to go with you. Even though you'd been horrible in the TV show you're still my best friend. Or at least you *were.*'

I'd tried to reply but she turned her back on me and strode over to Jason. He was cowering on the other side of the room, still whining that I was a total maniac who'd nearly killed him. Vanya hugged him **AGAIN!** Then she told him not to worry – that she would protect him from me. All the while, Trevor clapped his hands together and said things like, 'This is gonna make great telly!' and, 'Magic. Pure magic!'

Meanwhile, Rosie Taylor was staring at them, grinding her teeth together so hard I thought they might crumble out of her head.

Sitting in my bedroom a few hours later, I reflected on my terrible situation. I'd lost one of my best friends, who was now going to the prom with someone awful. My other best friend had landed me in mega trouble just so he could save himself from going to a school for naughty kids.

And worst of all, there were no flipping doughnuts in the house.

What was I going to do?

The Answer

It was about half five when the answer fell out of the sky.

Well, it smacked against my window anyway.

I screamed.

Darren Gamble's face was pressed against my skylight, his nose bent upwards so that a long snail trail of snot dragged across the glass.

I was so shocked I thought my head might fall off. 'How the crispy chicken nugget did you get up here?' I cried.

Let me explain something to you. My bedroom is in the attic of our house, so the windows are part of the roof. The roof! Ten metres up in the air with concrete and tarmac below.

'Let us in!' he called from outside.

What was going on?

Carefully, I stood on a chair to lift the latch. The window flipped up, and Gamble slithered through the gap and fell on to my floor. 'Hard work climbing that drainpipe, innit.'

'Why didn't you just knock on the front door?'

'Oh. Didn't think of that.'

I shook my head. 'You could've been killed.'

'Nah,' he scoffed, clearing his nose out and rubbing it into the carpet with his boot. 'I've climbed on to loads of roofs. I don't normally die.'

What a nutter!

'Why are you here?' I asked him. I noticed for the first time that he was wearing a shirt and a bow tie, and he seemed to have polished his head. He looked like a serial killer.

'Taking you to the prom,' he said, pulling me towards the window. 'Come on. I'm your fairy godmother.'

'Whoa whoa whoa,' I replied. 'I'm banned from going. And anyway, why would I want to?'

Gamble's whole body stiffened. His eyes narrowed to two dangerous slits and his voice dropped to a growl. 'I'm gonna sort Jason and Trevor out. And you're gonna help me.'

Gamble can flip like this over absolutely nothing. It's terrifying. Like that lunchtime when someone accidentally used his spoon. He went totally nuts and beat the kid up with a slice of melon and three grapes.

'Why do you want to get them?' I asked him.

He was now pacing up and down my room, punching my wall. 'Pair of snakes. They dropped me in it. Look . . .'

He held out his hand.

I knew straight away what it was – the object he'd snatched out of Mr Gibbons' hand on the field. The object that must've fallen out of my ear when Vanya punched me.

'The mind-control receiver,' I said. 'Just like on the army website.'

'I couldn't get hold of a hearing aid – I asked a load of deaf people, but none of 'em would give theirs to me.'

'Can't think why,' I sighed.

'So Trevor gave me this,' continued Gamble. 'It's the earpiece from that microphone Jason was wearing in the assembly. Only took ten minutes to twiddle some frequencies and add a couple of chips I got off the internet. Then I just had to program a quick app for Trevor's phone and off we went.'

At that moment, something clicked inside my head. 'Hang on,' I said. 'Are you some kind of super-brain genius?'

I couldn't believe that this had never crossed my mind before. But to be fair, why would it have? I mean, he's always more likely to *eat* a book than read it. His handwriting looks like a slug's been drowned in ink, then flicked across his page. The only lesson I've ever seen him pay attention in was about electricity. And even then, instead of wiring up a bulb to a battery, he just stuck his tongue in the plug socket in the wall and got blown halfway across the room 'for a laugh'.

But still, he *must* be pretty clever, maybe just not in a normal way. He'd outsmarted the school security system to put his fish in the pool. He'd hacked into the army website. He'd fixed Miss Clegg's car. And *now* he'd built his very own mind-control receiver out of an earphone.

Of course, he'd then used this receiver to turn me into a murderous maniac but still . . . you can't win them all, I guess.

Gamble shrugged again. 'People think I'm thick but I'm proper smart, me.'

'But how could you do that to me?' I said, after a while. 'I nearly killed him.'

'I'm sorry, mate,' he said, looking at me with his big eyes. 'I shouldn't have let Trevor control your brain like that. But I was desperate. Trevor said he'd put in a good word with Mr Gibbons so that I won't have to go to the bad-boy school. But afterwards he wouldn't. He said that he needed everyone to think it was your fault. If people found out it was me and him, then the TV show wouldn't work. He lied to me.'

I sighed. You can't stay mad at Gamble for long. It's not like he's a normal person, is it? The kid lists 'biting people' as one of his main interests.

'So that's two of us he's messed around with,' I said.

'And that's why we're gonna do summat about it,' he said, an evil glint in his eye. 'We're gonna fix him.'

I felt excited about this. Well, for about a second anyway. Until he picked up my shoes and threw them out of the window. I heard them land with a slap on the driveway below.

'What did you do that for?'

'We're going to the prom.'

'But I could've put them on downstairs, *then* gone out.'

He considered this for a moment. 'Oh yeah. I suppose you could.'

'Anyway. I'm not going anywhere. Even if I wanted to, I'm banned.'

'You *are* coming. I'm gonna get that Trevor. And you're gonna save Vanya, innit.'

One Question

I could totally understand why Gamble wanted to get Trevor. But, of course, I had one question: *what was I saving Vanya from?*

Oh, and what exactly *did he mean by* get *Trevor?*

And while I'm at it, *why did he want to help me to save Vanya?* Gamble hates Vanya – he's jealous of the fact we're friends. One lunchtime he put his pet dog Scratchy's bum worms into her stir-fried noodles.

OK, so strictly speaking I actually had three questions, but still . . .

'I feel bad about the brain controller, and I know you like her,' he said. 'Oh, and Jason's planning to kiss her!'

'What?!' I cried.

'Yeah,' said Gamble, 'remember they're going to have a prize for the best couple at the prom. Well, Trevor's gonna cheat so that Vanya and Jason win. Then the glitter cannon is gonna go off and Jason's gonna kiss her on stage in front of everyone!'

'Urgh, yuck!' I said. 'Why would anyone want to kiss another person? Even Vanya? Imagine the germs!'

Gamble scratched a spot on his scalp. 'It's the

big finale to the TV series. Trevor says they need an epic moment so everyone watching will go mad about it and buy all Jason's crummy music.'

This didn't quite make sense. 'But Vanya won't want to kiss him. It'll look awful on TV if he tries to kiss her and she storms off.'

'Doesn't matter. They can just freeze the screen before she does that. As long as he gets his lips on her gob with all the glitter coming down, then it'll look good.'

A terrible feeling came over me. I didn't feel like I could speak.

'So,' said Gamble, 'you coming or what?'

I suppose that everyone has times when they have to be brave or be a coward. Normally, I'm a coward. I'm scared of mice. I'm scared of salad. I'm scared of mice eating salad.

But today, I was brave.

'Yes,' I said finally.

'Wicked!' said Gamble, headbutting the door in celebration. Before I could stop him, he'd dived out of the window, run across the roof and disappeared down the drainpipe.

'You could've just used the stairs,' I called after him, shaking my head.

Racing to School

When I went downstairs, Mum was out in the back garden. I didn't want to lie to her about where I was going, but I didn't want her to be mad at me either. As a result, I decided to leave her the kind of note that she would find so unbelievably cute that she could never be mad at me (she is the most embarrassing person in the world, of course). So I wrote:

Gone out for a kiss. Back later.

Perfect. She didn't need to know that I was trying to *stop* a kiss, not *do* a kiss.

Once I'd left the note, I shot through the front door, ready to race to school.

However, as soon as I stepped outside and saw Gamble, I realised that *racing* into town wasn't going to be possible.

'What. Is *that*?' I asked him.

'It's my bike,' grinned Gamble.

'That is never yours.'

'Course it's mine,' he said. 'I nicked it from outside a shop.'

Why would I expect anything else? 'I'm not sure that's how it works.'

It was a woman's bike and it was absolutely MA-HOOOSSIVE. The woman who owned it must've been a flipping giant. The seat was almost as high as the top of Gamble's head.

And as if this wasn't bad enough, there was a trailer attached to the back of it. The trailer was one of those covered ones – like a buggy with a roof – that you see babies being towed in.

'Hop in and I'll pull you along,' grinned Gamble.

'I'll never fit!' I exclaimed. 'Those trailers are built for two-year-olds.'

'There's loads of space in there,' he said. 'When I pinched it off that woman, I had to tip both her kids on to the pavement before I could ride off.'

I slapped my hand over my face. Only Darren Gamble could chuck a couple of babies on to the hard ground so that he could steal a bicycle. 'I'm not going anywhere in that thing.'

'How else are you gonna get there? Prom's already started, innit.'

Huffing my cheeks, I stepped towards the trailer and pulled back the Velcro flap. And *oh my word.* 'Not a chance!'

There were two tiny seats inside the trailer. Both of them were already taken. One was filled by the sheep that Gamble had kidnapped the other day. The other one was taken up by Gamble's dog Scratchy.

I mentioned Scratchy before. Basically, Scratchy is one of the most disgusting creatures in the universe. It is made up of: 60 per cent bones, 10 per cent mangy fur, 10 per cent worms and fleas, and 20 per cent terrible smell.

'Why on earth have you brought Scratchy and a sheep?' I asked.

'The sheep's so I can ruin Trevor's TV show.'

'And Scratchy?'

Gamble shrugged. 'Just cos he's lovely!'

Scratchy bent its head forward under its seatbelt and licked its bum.

Gross. 'I am definitely not g–'

Before I could finish, Gamble shoved me in the back and I stumbled head first into the little trailer. He fastened the Velcro behind me and I was closed in, my legs dangling out of the side. It was horrible in there – tight and hot and stinky and claustrophobic. The space was so tiny that my face was centimetres from Scratchy's mouth. Its rotten breath was making me feel faint. Further down my body, the sheep was trying to eat my T-shirt.

'Hold on tight and enjoy the ride!' cried Gamble, struggling to pedal the bike. My legs dragged painfully along the tarmac.

Scratchy farted cheerfully.

Unpleasant Journey

The ride to school was the most unpleasant journey I've ever been on. It was even worse than the time I sat next to Kevin *Vomasaurus Retch* Harrison on the Spinning Twister of Terror at the funfair last year.

At first, Gamble struggled to get the enormous bike to move. We went about three metres in ten minutes. But things got much worse when he had the bright idea of holding on to the backs of cars and lorries, so they'd pull us along the road behind them.

WARNING: This is just about the stupidest and most dangerous thing you could ever do, and unless you enjoy being crushed to a painful death beneath the wheels of heavy vehicles, I'd suggest you don't try it yourself.

Of course, Gamble thought it was brilliant. He called it car-surfing. I called it stupid. The whole time, I could hear him in front shrieking: 'This is well good! We're all gonna die! Ha ha ha ha!'

I'm actually not quite sure how we *did* manage to survive. We were rocketing along the road at forty miles an hour, the trailer bouncing and swinging around all over the place. Several times we grazed against the wheels of a lorry or bumped into the side of a car.

In fact, the only way I could keep my legs from being torn off was to fold my body in half the wrong way, so my heels were high above the trailer and somewhere near the back of my head. Unfortunately, this position meant I had to bury my face way closer to Scratchy's bottom than was strictly healthy. And every time we went over a bump in the road, the disgusting mutt would let out a little parp right into my eyes.

It was horrible.

After what seemed like an eternity, we finally arrived at school. I was so relieved to still be alive that I scrambled out and kissed the tarmac.

'No time to snog the floor! Work to do!' Gamble

said, dragging me to my feet and pulling me across the playground.

Undesirables

The front of the school had been transformed. There was a long red carpet with potted plants either side of it leading to the main entrance, which now had a thick velvet curtain across it. A group of girls with 'WE LOVE YOU JASON' signs and flags were showing each other photos on their phones of when he'd walked past them.

Gamble and I strode on.

'Oh, look! Are *those two* famous people as well?' asked one of the girls.

'Nah,' replied her friend, 'just a couple of freaky-looking nobodies.'

Charming. Maybe they were friends of Rosie's.

We ran straight past them and up to the velvet curtain, when out stepped the biggest man I've ever seen. Seriously – he was the size of a bus, with muscles bulging out everywhere. He was standing behind a red rope that went from one side of the door to the other. As we went to lift the rope, he moved towards us.

'Who are you, you great big mutant?' asked Gamble. He's not afraid of anyone.

'Security,' grunted the great big mutant. He was wearing sunglasses and he didn't even look at us as he spoke. 'Keeping out undesirables.'

'What's undesirables?' asked Gamble.

Still not looking at us, the mutant pulled a piece of paper out of his pocket, unfolded it and held it up in front of our faces.

On it was printed the words: 'UNDESIRABLES! DO NOT LET THEM IN!' Underneath the writing were pictures of me and Gamble.

'Now hoppit!' said the mutant.

With a deafening battle cry, Gamble tried to charge past, but the mutant stepped in front of him. Gamble bounced off him like a pea being flicked against a wall.

Peeling himself off the floor, Gamble waved his fist at the mutant. 'I could smash your brains out but I ain't got time.'

The mutant stared straight ahead.

Gamble lowered his voice to me and led me away. 'I've got an idea.'

The Storeroom

'How am I supposed to get up there?' I asked, looking at the tiny window which was about six feet up the wall. From inside the building we could hear music and laughter.

'Easy,' said Gamble. He propped his bike against the wall. 'You can stand on my head. I've got a proper strong skull, me.'

He demonstrated this by picking up a loose brick and smashing it into tiny fragments on his forehead.

I tried to ignore this. 'And you're sure I'll be able to open it?'

'Course. I loosened the lock last year, so I can sneak in and out of school whenever I want.'

'Oh,' I said.

'Sometimes I come in at the weekend just to use the toilets and photocopy my bum.'

'Good grief,' I said. 'Right. Where does it lead to?'

'The PE store off the side of the hall,' he said. 'It's perfect, innit. We'll be able to sneak right into the prom without anyone seeing.'

I have to say this was pretty good thinking. 'So what's the plan when we get in there?'

'Nyah. We'll figure it out.'

'What do you m—' I began, but he'd already hoisted my foot so I had no choice but to scramble towards the window.

With a lot of heaving, clambering, shoving and slithering, I finally managed to squeeze through the window into the dark storeroom. Unfortunately, I hadn't really planned what I was going to do when I got through it. I grasped around frantically for something to grab hold of, but then Gamble gave my feet one last shove from below and I plunged head first to the ground with an agonising bump.

After about five seconds, I realised I wasn't actually dead, and I painfully stood up, banging my shoulder against a gymnastics bench. The little storeroom was dark, apart from the glow of disco lights underneath the curtain that leads to the hall. The music sounded much louder in here.

'I'm in,' I whispered up through the window. 'How are you going to get up?'

There was a long pause from outside. 'Oh. Hadn't thought of that,' said Gamble. 'Normally I bring a ladder, innit.'

I slapped my hand across my face. What had I been saying about Darren being a genius?

'I'll go find summat to climb up,' he said.

'Wait!' I said. 'Maybe I can pile up some gym apparatus and pull you up.'

But Darren didn't answer. He'd already gone.

I realised that I was alone. Or was I? A voice suddenly cut through the darkness from behind me.

'Oh-ho!' it said. 'Roman Garstang. So glad you could join us.'

I very slowly turned around. A torch shone directly into my eyes.

Rule Nine

'How did you know I was here?' I said, holding up my hands to block the dazzling light.

'I told everyone to look out for you,' replied Trevor calmly from behind the torch. 'That sicky kid Kevin went outside to puke just now. Said he'd seen you climbing through the window.'

Thanks a bunch, Vomasaurus Retch.

'Come to watch Jason kissing your little friend?' asked Trevor. His voice was cruel and mocking.

I gulped. He was blocking the exit, so there was no way out.

'Course you have,' he continued. 'Glad you're here to watch it. It's gonna make great TV. And, best of all, it's going to make YOU very, very upset indeed.'

'Eh?' I said. That wasn't very nice. 'Why would you want me to be upset?'

'You know who I am, don't you?'

Weird question. 'Trevor?' I offered.

He tutted. 'I'm Jason's *manager*. It's my job to make him rich and famous. And if he gets rich, he gives me half, then I become rich too.'

'I still don't get it.'

'You really *are* dumb, aren't you? When you showed your bum on TV, everyone voted for that sheep. You cost Jason the *BRT* final. And *that* cost me a lot of money. Do you know how much cash that juggling sheep made last year? Three million quid. *Three million!* What a waste! What can a sheep spend money on, eh? Gold-plated grass? That should've been Jason. Then *I* would've had half. This TV show is my chance to put Jason where he deserves to be. And to fill my pockets with lovely money. And if I can get back at you for what you did, then so much the better.'

'Oh,' I said.

Trevor was shining the torch underneath his chin now. It made his face look creepy and demonic. 'Jason blamed the sheep. He wanted to forgive you,' he said, ranting like a maniac now. 'But I kept telling him how evil you are. Kept him as angry with you as I could. Told him how you'd stolen money off us with your spotty little butt cheeks.'

I gulped. 'But . . .'

'Jason's too soft of course. That's his problem,' sneered Trevor. I got the impression that Trevor wasn't talking *to* me any more. He was just speaking out loud. 'He believes in *love* and *friendship* and *people's feelings.*'

He said these things like they were disgusting swear words.

'He didn't even want to take Vanya to the prom,' he went on. 'Said they were just good friends. Didn't want to upset her by kissing her. He loves that Rosie girl, see, but I said, *you can't have that one. The people watching at home won't like her. Take the other one – the nice one. The whole country will love it when you snog her onstage. And if you can turn her against that little rat, Roman, then so much the better.* It's worked perfectly so far.'

I remembered that conversation I'd overheard Trevor and Jason having earlier in the week.

'But you're using people,' I said.

'Great, isn't it!' he said. 'Rule nine of a great TV show: know everything about everyone, then use it. Like your little mate. As soon as I saw he needed a good report off that Mr Gibbons, I knew I could get him to help me this afternoon.'

'That's horrible,' I said.

'Yes, it was, wasn't it,' he replied proudly. 'But not as horrible as this is going to be for you.'

He pulled out his phone. The screen glowed in the darkness.

'Yep. Ready to roll,' he said into it, then hung up. 'Watch through the curtain, Roman. You're going to love this.'

He pushed me to the edge of the curtain, then stood behind me, firmly holding me in place by both of my shoulders. The walls of the hall were covered in long billowing sheets so it resembled a giant tent. There was a DJ in the corner and disco lights spinning round everywhere. The curtain was right alongside a stage. In the middle of it stood the glitter cannon that they'd used at the launch of Spaghetti Grooves.

The dance-floor was pretty much empty in the middle. The boys were mainly standing against one wall, the girls against the other. They were all looking towards the centre of the room.

Because of Trevor's hand on my shoulder, I couldn't move. But even if I'd wanted to, I was frozen to the spot.

Everybody was watching Jason and Vanya, who were dancing together. They were holding hands, and now he was spinning her around and now he was backflipping and now she was body-popping and, worst of all, they were both smiling.

It was awful.

But things got worse.

The lights came on and Rosie Taylor strutted on to the stage and stood next to the glitter cannon. She was wearing a long white dress with a train that dragged for miles along the floor behind her. In one hand she held a sparkly gold envelope. In the other, she had a microphone.

'Good evening, fans,' she beamed. 'And now the moment you've all been waiting for – we're going to announce the winners of the couple of the year contest!'

Everyone started cheering and whooping. The

girls and boys reluctantly shuffled together into pairs.

'Why is Rosie so happy?' I said. 'I thought she was fuming about Jason not taking her to the prom.'

'Told you. Rule nine,' said Trevor, 'know everything about everyone. She's desperate to be famous and on TV but nobody asked her to the prom. Came to me this afternoon begging to do this job. Even said she'd operate the glitter cannon for us. That miserable teacher wouldn't do it, see.'

I looked around the room for Mrs McDonald. She was nowhere to be seen. Miss Clegg was in the corner talking at Mr Gibbons. He must've come here to see Gamble.

'And so,' grinned Rosie, onstage, 'let's find out who the winners are . . .'

The camerawoman edged on to the stage. Rosie slowly opened the envelope.

I frowned. Something about this whole thing didn't make sense. I mean, Trevor said that he knew everything about Rosie, but this was not like her at all. If she's angry with someone, she always gets revenge, no matter what they've done. One time, I accidentally lost the lid of her gel pen. To get me back, she paid a professional graffiti artist to draw a ten-metre-tall picture of me in the nude on a wall opposite the school.

There was no way in a million years that she'd let Jason go to the prom with Vanya without doing something to them in return. But what was she planning?

The Glitter Cannon

'Oh, I am *SOOOO* pleased for this couple!' exclaimed Rosie, holding the envelope to her chest. 'Hashtag: *how sweet*. The couple of the year are . . .'

There was a long drum roll, which seemed to go on for ages. Rosie moved backwards slightly so that she was next to the glitter cannon.

Then something made me turn around. Maybe it was a noise from the window. I'm not sure. But as I turned, I noticed the light glinting against something next to me.

I squinted in the darkness. *What was that?* I had to reach forward to open the curtain slightly further. A little more light sneaked in and oh my word!

By my feet was a massive pile of empty tins of Spaghetti Grooves. There must've been about twenty of them, all dripping with disgusting orange sauce.

I shot my eyes back towards the stage. And then I noticed Rosie gently easing the barrel of the glitter cannon downwards so it was pointing across the stage. She did it slowly – millimetre by millimetre - so that nobody would've noticed unless they were watching carefully.

'Vanya Goyal and JASON GROOVES!' cried Rosie.

The crowd went wild. Jason and Vanya made their way to the stage.

'And now for the kiss!' hissed Trevor into my ear.

I'd almost forgotten he was there. And in any case, I wasn't bothered about the kiss any more. Because Vanya and Jason were now onstage. And Rosie was standing right behind the glitter cannon. And I had realised exactly what she was planning to do with it.

The cannon.

The tins.

Rosie must've put them there. *I even got my dad to buy two hundred tins to sell at his shopping centre.*

Good grief.

'FIVE . . .' she called out, and the crowd joined in . . . 'FOUR . . .'

'NOOOOO!' I screamed.

I tried to break free but Trevor clamped his hand on my shoulder even more tightly.

'THREE . . .'

'But you don't underst–'

'Shut your face and watch it, you little turd. You deserve this. As soon as that cannon goes off, he's going to give her a peck. And after that, who cares. I've got my big ending.'

'TWO . . .'

This was terrible.

But then Gamble's dog, Scratchy, fell from the sky.

Seriously. It came tumbling down from above like a big filthy snowflake. And then Gamble's face was at the window. 'Get him, boy!' he cried. He must've found something to stand on and shoved Scratchy through from outside.

'What the . . .' exclaimed Trevor, as Scratchy charged at him. Then he let out a loud 'OOOOOFFFFFFF' as the dog gave him a flying headbutt to the *you-know-wheres*. His phone skittered off across the floor and clanged against the tins of Spaghetti Grooves.

Meanwhile, Gamble was huffing and puffing with something outside the window.

I didn't have time to worry about that though. Trevor was now lying doubled up on the floor and I was free.

'ONE . . .'

During the next second, lots of things happened.

Rosie reached for the button on the glitter cannon, which was now pointing directly at Vanya and Jason without them realising.

I leapt on to the stage and charged across it.

Jason leaned towards Vanya, who didn't seem to have noticed.

Rosie put one finger in her ear and pushed down the button.

There was a loud KABOOM!

And I dived forward, right in front of the cannon, as twenty tins' worth of Spaghetti Grooves came blasting out and crashed into my chest, flinging me backwards.

Silence

The force of the Spaghetti Grooves had blown me halfway across the stage and I'd smacked my head against the wall. Completely dazed, I was sprawled out in a giant puddle of sauce and millions of tiny pasta Jasons. There was a ringing sound in my ears, and the world was spinning. My skin stung, like when you stand too close to a fire, and I couldn't move.

Rosie, Vanya and Jason were looking down at me.

'He's not dead,' said Rosie. She seemed quite disappointed about this.

'Roman. You . . . saved me,' said Vanya.

I tried to speak but I'd been winded by the spaghetti bomb and I could barely breathe. Once again, I felt my eyes painfully closing as they swelled up from the hot sauce.

'Quick!' cried Trevor from the side of the stage. He was still doubled over in pain. 'Kiss her! Kiss her!'

'Do *what*?' asked Vanya, looking at Jason. 'But I said . . .'

'It's for the TV show . . .' Jason murmured.

'But you said we were friends.' Vanya backed away, but slipped on the sauce and fell on her backside. And now Jason was standing over her, the camerawoman right next to him.

'Do it!' cried Trevor, still lying on the ground.

Where was Gamble? Only he could stop this now.

Jason moved forward.

Vanya tried to back away but there was nowhere to go.

And then something amazing happened.

From nowhere, the sheep came barrelling on to the stage. Its eyes were glazed and lifeless like a zombie's. It ran – no, *hurtled* – at Jason, just as his lips were about to touch Vanya's cheek.

The sheep butted him right up the backside and sent him flying off the side of the stage, sprawling into the audience below.

And there was Gamble, behind it, with Trevor's mobile in his hand and a great big grin on his face. 'Put the brain controller in its car, innit.'

Gamble wiggled his finger. I was pretty spaced out at this moment, so I may have imagined this, but I'm pretty sure that the sheep began moon-walking across the stage, drabbing its front hooves.

And now Vanya had me by the shoulders. 'Quick!' she yelled. 'Help! Someone needs to wash this hot sauce off my best friend.'

And that was the last thing I heard before I passed out.

Epilogue

I was completely unconscious for the next five minutes, so everything that happened next was told to me by other people.

Luckily, my mum had read the note about the kiss. Being the most embarrassing person on earth, she'd rushed straight to the school along with my dad and his video camera, hoping to 'catch the beautiful moment when I laid my lips on a lucky young lady'. *YUCK!*

They arrived just as I was fainting onstage. Apparently, Gamble tried to give me the kiss of life, so I'm glad I was unconscious. Mum always carries a massive packet of wet wipes around with her (in case I 'have a little accident'), so she was able to clean the sauce off before it did too much damage.

Rosie was seriously angry with Jason for trying to kiss Vanya. She told him he was dumped. 'Hashtag: *it's over*,' she apparently said. 'I'm gonna find me a real celebrity boyfriend.'

Nobody else thought that Jason seemed too bothered. Firstly, I don't think he knew that they were going out with each other in the first place. Secondly, he was too busy being pinned down by the sheep, which Gamble was controlling to kiss him again and again on the face. Jason was crying for help from Trevor, but he'd already sneaked off, never to be seen again.

When I finally came round, this had all already happened, and the prom was over. Mum took me home and treated me to a full-on double doughnut extravaganza. Vanya and Gamble came along too. They both enjoyed the food but Gamble was made to eat outside after he insisted on bringing Scratchy and the sheep with him.

The TV programme never got shown, and very soon, Jason went back to being plain old Kenneth Shufflebottom. However, Simon Bowel did like some of the shots they'd got of Gamble. Keep your eyes peeled for his one-off special: *Britain's Naughtiest Kid*. It'll be on some Freeview channel next year, showing all of the outrageous stunts he pulled that week.

Which reminds me, of course. Mr Gibbons finally finished his report and Gamble WILL be going to the normal high school with me in September. According to him, Gamble 'might have a lot of energy' and a 'mischievous spirit'. But he is an 'extremely intelligent boy' with 'amazing technical skills' who will 'do anything to help anyone'.

Who knew?

MARK LOWERY grew up in Preston but now lives near Cambridge with his young family. Some of the time he is a primary-school teacher. In the olden days he used to do lots of active stuff like running, hiking, snowboarding and swimming, but now he prefers staying in and attempting to entertain his children. He plays the guitar badly and speaks appalling Italian, but he knows a lot about biscuits. In his mind he is one of the great footballers of his generation, although he is yet to demonstrate this on an actual football pitch. He has an MA in Writing for Children and his first two books – *Socks Are Not Enough* and *Pants Are Everything* – were both shortlisted for the Roald Dahl Funny Prize. Mark is also the author of the Roman Garstang series (*The Jam Doughnut that Ruined My Life*; *The Chicken Nugget Ambush*; *The Attack of the Woolly Jumper*; *The Great Caravan Catastrophe*) and *Charlie and Me: 421 Miles from Home*. He is yet to find a cake that he doesn't like.

Follow Mark at www.marklowery.co.uk or on Twitter: @hellomarklowery

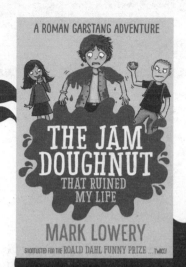

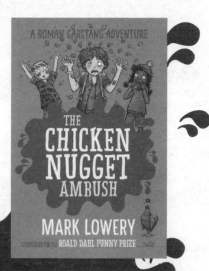

READ ALL THE ROMAN GARSTANG ADVENTURES!

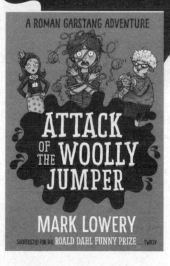

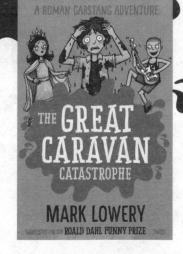

Thank you for choosing a Piccadilly Press book.

If you would like to know more about our authors, our books or if you'd just like to know what we're up to, you can find us online.

www.piccadillypress.co.uk

You can also find us on:

We hope to see you soon!